Dakota Chase

Repeating History:
The Eye of Ra
Dakota Chase

Illustrations by Kiernan Kelly

Prizm Books
a subsidiary of Torquere Press, Inc.

Repeating History: The Eye of Ra
This is a work of fiction. Names, characters, places, and incidents either are the product of the author's imagination or are used fictitiously. While this novel is inspired by historical events, it is a fictionalized portrayal, and the author created all characters, events and storylines in the pursuit of literary fiction, not historical accuracy.

Repeating History: The Eye of Ra
PRIZM
An imprint of Torquere Press, Inc.
PO Box 2545
Round Rock, TX 78680
Copyright 2010 © by Dakota Chase
Cover illustration by Kiernan Kelly
Published with permission
ISBN: 978-1-60370-983-5
www.prizmbooks.com
www.torquerepress.com

All rights reserved, which includes the right to reproduce this book or portions thereof in any form whatsoever except as provided by the U.S. Copyright Law. For information address Torquere Press. Inc., PO Box 2545, Round Rock, TX 78680.
First Prizm Printing: May 2010
Printed in the USA

If you purchased this book without a cover, you should be aware the this book is stolen property. It was reported as "unsold and destroyed" to the publisher, and neither the author nor the publisher has received any payment for this "stripped book".

www.prizmbooks.com

Repeating History:
The Eye of Ra
Dakota Chase

Illustrations by Kiernan Kelly

Repeating History: The Eye of Ra

Chapter One

When the gavel hit the small oval of polished wood on the bench as the judge called the court to order, the sound rolled through the courtroom like a thunderbolt. I flinched and glanced up at the ceiling, half-expecting to see black storm clouds boiling up under the eaves.

I shifted uncomfortably in my seat. The courtroom was crowded with juvenile offenders, and it would be a good, long while before my name was called. I was at the far end of the alphabet, under the "W's," at least when going by last names. First names are another story, but hardly anybody lists people by first names.

Aston Walsh. That's me.

I supposed I should've been used to it all by now. After all, I was a seasoned professional. It was my third trip before the Honorable James Fredrick of Eastman County, an old man who looked like somebody's grandfather, and probably was, but who had a sneer perpetually plastered on his doughy face. Twice before, I'd been arrested and charged with vandalism of school property, ending up in his courtroom.

Spraying graffiti on the walls of Roosevelt High had seemed like a good idea at the time, but I'd been caught red-handed both times with the paint still wet on my hands. I can't even remember why I did it, aside from sheer boredom, but then I'd never really needed a good, solid reason to do anything, stupid or otherwise. I was always a sort of a spur-of-the-moment kind of guy.

My first offense got me a slap on the wrist and a warning from the judge. The second time earned me a summer doing community service by picking up trash five days a week in Danhart Lake Park. My court-appointed lawyer told me I was lucky to have gotten off so easily.

Lucky? Yeah, right. Being sentenced to nine weeks chiseling old chewing gum off park benches, picking up trash, and hosing smelly slime out of garbage cans was just as good as winning a trip to Disneyworld, right? Lucky, lucky me.

Still, I had to admit—at least to myself, since I'd rather cut off my right arm than admit *any* adult might be right where I was concerned, particularly a pasty-faced worm like my court-appointed lawyer—it could've been worse. I might have drawn a "Go directly to jail, do not pass Go, do not collect two hundred dollars" card. The judge could've sent me to Juvenile Hall, or worse, I could've been tried as an adult and sent to prison. Neither was somewhere that scored highly on my list of places I most wanted to visit, so in that regard, yeah, I was lucky.

You see, I have a thing about being confined. *Claustrophobia* is what they call it. Lock me in a small place where I'm unable to get out quickly, and I fall to pieces. Trust me, it isn't pretty. My heart starts hammering; I break out into a cold sweat, and I start shaking. The experience usually ends with me puking up last week's breakfast.

Told you it wasn't pretty.

My father sat next to me on the wooden bench. He

worked in construction, and it showed in his big, rough hands. They were scarred and callused, and the skin on the back of his neck was always sunburned. My dad was a big man, beefy, and looked ridiculously uncomfortable in his rumpled dress shirt and black tie. The only other times I could remember my dad wearing a tie was at my mother's funeral, and when he married my stepmom. Neither was an occasion I liked to think about.

My dad wouldn't look at me. He was staring straight at the wall at the front of the courtroom, and his expression was stony. Every so often, he muttered something under his breath that I couldn't quite hear.

I had no problem imagining what he was saying, though.

"Thank God your mother didn't live to see you now… a common criminal… what a disappointment."

The words, real or imagined, cut through me like a knife. My father wasn't talking about Alice, my stepmother. No, my dad was talking about my real mother. She'd died several years ago, when I was just ten years old, and nothing had been the same since, especially since my dad remarried.

I don't like to think about my real mom if I can help it. It hurts too much.

Alice, Dad's second wife, refused to come to court at all, although I didn't see that as a big loss. She rarely noticed me anyway, except to complain about something I'd done or not done. She just didn't like me, never had, and the feeling was more than mutual. I didn't miss having her there at all, but my real mom? That was another story.

I felt my eyes burn, and swallowed a lump in my throat. My stomach churned with the anger that always seemed to boil up when I thought about my mom. I really,

really missed her, especially at times like these. I loved her more than I could say, and I hated her at the same time for leaving me.

Stupid, right? I mean, I know that people can't help dying. It happens to everybody sooner or later, but knowing it didn't make a difference. I still blamed her and felt like she deserted me.

Thinking about my mom was really painful and didn't help my mood one bit. My hands curled into fists, squeezing until my nails bit sharply into my palms. *Keep it up, Aston, and you'll have a full-blown panic attack right here and now.* The last thing I wanted to do in a courtroom full of possible cellmates was show them how frightened I was. I forced my attention to the others in the room with me, trying to distract myself from my screaming nerves.

Teenagers filled the benches around me, most sitting next to adults; some looked scared, others angry, and a few bored. I spotted two who were crying and another who look as if he was about to hurl.

A few kids appeared to have their own lawyers, like the dark-haired kid dressed in a sharp blue suit in the front row. *Money talks,* I thought snidely. I didn't have a private lawyer. My attorney was court-appointed and was representing fifty kids that day. He barely knew my name. I got the feeling that I was just a case number to him, a paycheck, and that sucked because I was sure I wouldn't get much in the way of a defense. Not that I had any—I'd done the deed, and once again, had been caught red-handed—but it would've been nice to have somebody who didn't think I was a total loser.

I nervously chewed on my bottom lip and drummed my fingers against my thigh to a beat inside my head as

I watched a kid represented by the same court-appointed attorney sentenced to six months at the Havenwood Juvenile Detention Facility. I felt a cold shiver, wondering if I would be sitting next to him in the van heading to Havenwood that afternoon.

According to what I'd heard, Havenwood was a labor farm. Kids went in and got put to work hoeing fields and digging holes and stuff.

Six months' hard labor for a first offense? The judge was in a foul mood today. His bushy white eyebrows knit together, looking like a single white, fuzzy caterpillar stretching across his forehead. As I watched, he remanded no less than ten kids into the custody of the state, all to Havenwood, and for crimes a lot less serious than mine.

That was the very moment that killed whatever hope I might've had. Things were going to be bad for me this time, and I might—just *might*—be seriously screwed.

Okay, definitely screwed, and big time.

Like it'd been with the graffiti, stealing the car had *seemed* like a good idea at the time, but looking back, I couldn't figure out why. After all, I had no plans to keep it or sell it, only to drive it around for a while. It seemed ridiculous to me now, sitting in court waiting for my turn, that I'd risked my freedom for a fifteen-minute joyride in a shiny black BMW.

Of course, I'd never considered the fact that I might be *caught*, either. I never did.

Which is why this was my third trip before the Honorable James Frederick. *Three strikes and you're out*, I thought, watching another boy step up before the judge. It was the dark-haired kid in the blue suit, the one who had his own lawyer.

Grant Reginald William Vaughn was the kid's name.

No wonder he has his own lawyer, I thought. *If he can afford four names, he can afford his own attorney. That's just perfect. Rich boy will get probation and I'll probably get the chair.*

I saw a man I assumed was his father sitting next to him and his lawyer. The pretty young girl on his other side must've been his sister or girlfriend. She looked like she could've been a model—skinny, perfect, and blonde.

Didn't it figure?

Vaughn didn't get probation, but he also wasn't sent to Juvie, either. He was found guilty of breaking and entering, and sentenced to a year at the Stanton School for Boys, a place I'd never heard of before.

Still has to beat going to Juvie, I thought. *I can smell my own bacon sizzling already. The last time I was in here, the judge said if he saw me in his courtroom one more time, I was done for. I'll be wearing a freaking orange jumpsuit by dinnertime.*

"Aston Walsh."

I blinked, startled to hear my own name, even though I'd been sitting there, anticipating it. It was my turn at the bench. In an instant, I forgot all about Grant Reginald William Vaughn with his four names, blue suit, and fancy lawyer, and was consumed by fear for my own future. Would I be going home tonight with my dad or riding in the white county van to Juvenile Hall? My feet dragged as I stood up and followed my dad to the head of the room, standing next to the balding, bored, court-appointed attorney.

"According to my records, this is your third arrest, young man. What do you have to say for yourself?" The judge's eyes were blue and diamond hard, glaring at me from across the bench. He no longer looked like somebody's grandfather. He looked like a man who could chew up and spit out a kid like me without thinking twice about it.

"I'm really sorry. I won't do it again." It sounded weak, even to me, but I actually meant it this time. *Please God, get me out of this and I swear I'll never break the law again. I won't even jaywalk. I'll be a model citizen. I'll obey traffic signals and help little old ladies cross the street.*

"Grand Theft Auto is a serious offense. You're lucky you haven't been charged as an adult. You'd be facing a possible sentence of up to ten years in the penitentiary. If it were in my power, I'd send you there anyway."

I gulped, feeling a sharp stab of fear lace through me, icy cold. Penitentiary! That was serious business. I doubted I could survive Juvie, never mind the pen. I felt the hot burn of tears at the back of my eyes. *Don't cry, don't cry,* I thought frantically, resisting the urge to swipe at my eyes and nose with my sleeve.

"However, you've been charged as a juvenile, and that limits my choices. I have several letters from your teachers attesting to your character, regardless of your lapse of common sense. Your grades are excellent, and despite your previous obsession with spray-painting obscenities on school property, you've attended class regularly. Therefore, I'm sentencing you to one year at the Stanton School for Boys. It's a private school outside of the city. You will report there at eight a.m. Monday morning."

He pointed his gavel at me, frowning. "Don't think you're getting off lightly, because you're not. Stanton is barely one step up from Juvenile Hall. The only difference is the uniform and the academic excellence. The school has been more than generous in contracting to take in boys who would otherwise end up in the penal system.

I'm giving you one last chance. Screw up, find yourself standing in front of me again, and I assure you that your next address will be a cell in Havenwood Penitentiary."

The gavel banged again, sounding even more like thunder than before, but I actually felt relieved.

Stanton School for Boys. It was just another high school, sort of like a summer sleep-away camp, right? I could handle this.

How bad could it be?

Chapter Two

I spent my last weekend of freedom incarcerated in my room, visited only by my dad and Alice. Not even my stepsisters, Alice's daughters, Beth and Tiffany, bothered to give me grief. Neither of my parents seemed particularly eager to spend time with me, and the feeling was totally mutual. There was a cold, uncomfortable barrier between us now, a thick, high wall built of my mistakes.

My dad subjected me to a repeat of every lecture he'd ever given me over the years, from the *"You Have So Much Potential"* sermon, to his trademarked *"Thank God Your Poor Mother Isn't Alive To See You Now,"* and the ever popular *"Where Did I Go Wrong?"* speeches. Alice stood nearby during all of them, wringing her hands and shaking or nodding her head in all the right places, like she was doing some sort of bizarre interpretive dance.

I didn't respond to any of them. I knew better than that. If I mouthed off, all it would get me was more of the same, except louder and longer than before. It was easier to shut up and stay that way.

Monday came almost as a relief. My dad delivered me to the Admissions Office of the Stanton School for Boys at seven a.m., signed his name on the dotted line, and left me there with one last parting order.

"Don't screw this up."

As if I'd planned on launching into an act of vandalism as soon as he turned his back on me.

Really, I thought with some contempt. Did I look like *that* much of a moron? I planned to wait at least a week before defacing any school property or mooning the principal.

Just kidding.

Actually, I had every intention of being the best-behaved student they'd ever had enrolled there. I would be seen, but heard only when asked a question. I would answer my teachers respectfully. I would do all of my homework. I would *not* make trouble. I would be a ghost. I would emerge from the Stanton School for Boys at the end of a year's time a changed man, with my diploma in my hand and my juvenile record sealed.

Yeah, and someday elephants would crap lollipops on the White House lawn.

For all my good intentions, it actually took me *less* than twenty-four hours to get into the worst trouble of my entire life.

But I'm getting ahead of myself.

After my dad left, I was called into the principal's office. Principal Martin Meek was everything but what his name implied. He was huge, for one thing, a giant of a man nearly as big around as he was tall. His chair creaked ominously when he sat down, and I winced at a mental image of it falling apart underneath him as if it were made of matchsticks.

It's a good thing I didn't laugh, or even crack a smile, because it soon became apparent that Principal Meek was born without a sense of humor. His bushy black eyebrows met in a frown, and stayed that way all through our interview.

I think it's safe for me to say that the only thing bigger than Principal Meek's waistline was his ego. It was a whopper.

The walls of Meek's office were papered with framed photographs and newspaper articles about…well, *Meek*. There was Meek posing with the mayor, Meek cutting the ribbon at the opening of the new library, and Meek with his arms around a few students. There were articles with headlines like, *"Martin Meek Helps Troubled Youth,"* and *"Martin Meek Given Humanitarian Award,"* and *"Martin Meek Receives Key to City."*

Meek, Meek, Meek.

I wondered how anyone could spend their days staring at photographs of themselves. Then Meek began to talk, and I thought I understood.

He was completely, unquestionably in love with himself. He probably blew kisses to the photographs of himself when nobody was looking.

"When I was a boy, I was a paragon of virtue, a credit to my community. I was never in trouble with the law, never spoke out of turn, and always showed the utmost respect for my elders. Then again, my father was a strict disciplinarian who would tolerate no shenanigans from my brothers or me, and I learned self-control at his knee. When I became principal here at the Stanton School for Boys, I was determined that I would help poor, misguided youth—like yourself—to become productive members of society by employing those same standards of discipline."

If he were any more full of himself, he'd be inside out.

I shrugged mentally. *He's just one more snobby teacher convinced of his own importance,* I thought. *I can handle him. Piece of cake.*

I realized I was wrong about him when he narrowed

his eyes at me, leaned over the desk (as much as his hugely rounded stomach would allow, anyway, which wasn't all that far), and hissed, "*That's* what I tell your parents, and what I tell the newspapers, and the teachers, and the mayor. *This* is what I tell my students privately: you get one shot, Walsh. I get five thousand bucks from the state per head to take troubled kids in. That money is the school's to keep regardless of whether you make it in here or not. Personally, I'd be just as happy to kick your butt out after the first day, and get another five grand for taking in the next punk. So go ahead and do me a favor... screw up. It'll just free up your bed for the next loser."

He sat back, glaring at me, daring me to say anything. For once, I was smart and kept my mouth shut.

He wasn't in love with himself. Well, he *was*, but he was also in love with making money, and he'd found his cash cow in the juvenile justice system. I wondered if it might not have been better for me to go to Juvie instead of the Stanton School for Boys. I had the feeling my stay here was not going to be as easy as I'd thought.

One thick finger stabbed the intercom button on his telephone console. "Mrs. Robeson? Kindly give our new boy, Mr. Walsh, his schedule and dorm room assignment, will you? Have one of the other students show him around campus before his first class."

Mrs. Robeson's squeaky voice answered. "Of course, Mr. Meek."

He sat back in his chair and shuffled a few papers, never looking in my direction again. "Well? What are you waiting for, Walsh, an engraved invitation? Get going."

I jumped up from the chair and launched myself out of the door before he could finish his sentence. I was many things, but an idiot wasn't one of them.

Okay, maybe I was an idiot at times, most times in fact, but not then.

I took his hint and got gone, practically sprinting back to the outer office.

Mrs. Robeson was middle-aged and paper-thin, giving the impression that she had a front and back, but no sides. I got the feeling that if she should turn sideways, she might disappear altogether. Her eyes were sharp, and they scanned me head to foot. She sniffed, obviously displeased with what she saw, then slid a piece of paper toward me. "This is your class schedule. Memorize it. Copy it. Tattoo it to your forehead. Do whatever you need to do to make sure you know where and when your classes are. Do *not* come to me to ask for a second copy, because you won't get one. I have better things to do with my time than print out copies of schedules all day long."

Somehow, I seriously doubted she had *anything* better to do, but again, showing tremendous restraint and remarkable good sense, I kept my mouth shut.

She made a phone call and asked someone named Mr. Hoovers to send someone named Mr. Peters down to the office, then looked at me. "Mr. Peters will be here directly to show you to your dorm room." She glanced at my schedule. "You have history with Mr. Ambrosius at one-fifteen in Room 110. Don't be late." With one last disdainful sniff, she turned her back on me.

I resisted the urge to wad up the schedule and ping it off the back of her head. *Two points! The crowd goes wild!* I thought, laughing on the inside.

What a witch. She seemed to be nothing but a slender, feminine version of the principal. *Meek-Lite,* I thought.

Well, I was two-for-oh. I'd met two people at my new school so far, and detested both on sight.

"Mr. Peters" turned out to be a tall, skinny boy my own age, with bad skin and a shock of hair so orangey-red it made him look like a lit match. He also didn't look happy to be appointed as Chief Tour Guide for New Guys at the Stanton School for Boys. His lip curled when he looked at me. "Come on," he said, "I don't have all day."

I followed the Human Torch out of the office, down a long corridor, and outside. We crossed a perfect square of neatly cut, emerald green grass. There were six buildings clustered around the Green, and all of them looked almost exactly alike. They were each three stories tall, with red brick walls and gray-tiled roofs.

My dorm room, 337A, was a tiny square painted stark white, with dark gray carpeting, and reminded me more of a cell than a bedroom. It was filled with two beds minus headboards, two four-drawer dressers, and two writing desks. The communal bathroom was located out in the hall. I half-expected to see bars on the single, narrow window, but all that covered it was a tan, roll-down shade.

My new roommate was nowhere in sight, although his suitcases were lined up neatly by one of the beds. They all matched, looked brand new, and were monogrammed neatly in gold.

G.R.W.V.

Those initials rang a bell, and I suddenly knew who owned the luggage.

Grant Reginald William Vaughn.

Mr. Four-Name-Blue-Suit-Private-Attorney from court was my new roommate. *Well*, I thought. *Lucky, lucky me.*

"You've got five minutes to make it to Mr. Ambrosius' World History class. It's in that building," Peters said, interrupting my train of thought. He was standing at the window, pulling the shade to the side and pointing a long, skinny finger across the Green at one of the other buildings. His lip curled in a sneer. "You'd better get the lead out or you'll be late, and Ambrosius *hates* students who are tardy."

My running total of people met and disliked on sight went up to three. So far, my day was shaping up to be a shut-out.

I was only slightly out of breath by the time I ran outside and across the Green to the building on the far side. I flung open the door and dashed down the hall, skidding to a stop in front of Room 110. Gathering my courage and pasting on my game face—my patented, slightly sour, slightly bored, slightly don't-want-to-be-here-but-they're-making-me face—I stepped inside.

"And you are...?" The voice was strong and sure, and at odds with the old man to whom it belonged. His skin was so thin it appeared transparent, dotted with brown spots and creased with age. A shock of white hair covered his scalp like a snowfall that matched his full beard, but he had clear, brilliant blue eyes, and his intense gaze pinned me in place. I couldn't have moved had I wanted to. His glare was so sharp I was sure it was drawing blood wherever it touched my skin.

"Uh..."

"Heavens, that's quite an unusual name. Your parents must've disliked you on sight. Class, please welcome Mr. Uh. Well, Uh, I suggest you take a seat. Back there, next to Mr. Vaughn."

I frowned as Ambrosius unconsciously threw my own thoughts back at me. Hadn't I thought the same thing about Meek, Robeson, and Peters? That I disliked them on sight? *Weird,* I thought, as I made my way to the back of the classroom and took a seat next to a vaguely familiar, dark-haired boy. It was Vaughn, he of the four names, suit, lawyer, and luggage.

We weren't only roommates—we probably had the same class schedule as well.

Terrific. We were going to be joined at the freaking hip.

I felt a little smug as I cast a vindictive little glare in his direction. All the money in the world hadn't kept him from ending up in exactly the same dump as me.

He returned my gaze with a surly one of his own.

Jerk.

I turned my attention back to Ambrosius.

"Since you, Mr. Uh, do not have a textbook, and I have given my last extra book to Mr. Vaughn, who came in just before you, you may share with him," Ambrosius said. "Please turn to page sixty-three of our texts. Yesterday, I believe we were reading about the Phoenicians." He scanned the room and, much to my relief, chose someone on the other side of it to begin reading.

I wondered how long the "Mr. Uh" thing would last before Ambrosius grew tired of his weak, little joke. Knowing my luck, I was probably doomed to be "Mr. Uh" for the rest of the school year.

Vaughn didn't seem any more enthusiastic about sharing with me than I felt, but I wasn't going to argue with Ambrosius on my first day in class. I'd already been labeled "Mr. Uh." I didn't want Ambrosius to add "The Pain in the Rump" to the title, which I was sure he'd do instantly if I asked to be moved.

Ambrosius launched into a long lecture about the Phoenicians, which I tuned out after about two and a half seconds. I picked at my nails and glanced periodically at the clock. I noticed Vaughn was paying no more attention than me. He was fiddling with a button on his Rolex.

Rolex? Jeez.

What teenager has a freaking *Rolex?* I wondered if it was real, then remembered his four names and his private attorney, and figured it was.

Life just wasn't fair.

Then Vaughn's elbow dug into my side. I began to snarl at him before I realized Ambrosius was talking to me.

"Mr. Uh, perhaps you would care to share with us two of the most significant contributions of the Phoenicians to civilization?"

"Uh..."

"Yes, we've already established that as your name." There was a twittering among the other students, and I felt my ears and cheeks grow hot. I hated to be laughed at.

At least, I did when the joke was on me and not of my own making.

"Mr. Casey," Ambrosius said, nodding toward a boy on the opposite side of the classroom, "perhaps you can tell us?"

I noticed Casey sat up straight and smiled, as if pleased to be called on.

Suck up.

"The alphabet and circumnavigation."

"Very good, Mr. Casey." Ambrosius directed his fiery blue gaze at me again. "You will find that I take history very seriously, Mr. Uh. Only by understanding the lessons of the past can we succeed in the future."

My cheeks blazed. I hated being the brunt of a joke,

hated more being singled out in front of the class. I was new, for corn's sake! You'd think he'd have a little pity and cut me some slack on my first day. At that moment, all the good intentions I'd had went sailing out of my head. I opened my mouth and my tongue started flapping. "The past is gone, man. *Now* is all that matters. There's nothing I need to learn from a bunch of old dead guys. They didn't have cars or computers, and since I don't think I'll be in a swordfight or trying to sail around the world anytime soon, there's nothing they can teach me."

"Truth, dude," Vaughn said. I hadn't expected him to be a supporter, but was grateful I wasn't alone. We knuckle-bumped to celebrate our newfound camaraderie. Maybe Mr. Blue Suit wasn't going to be such a bad roomie after all.

It wasn't until I looked back at Ambrosius that the thought occurred to me that I might have just made a big mistake. His eyes were crackling with fury, his bushy white eyebrows knit in a frown. "Poet and philosopher George Santayana once said, 'Those who cannot remember the past are condemned to repeat it.' Those are wise words, gentlemen. I'd suggest you both ponder their meaning while you wait for me in my office." His eyes narrowed and pointed toward the door. "Go. *Now.*"

Oh, man. I'm not in class fifteen minutes, and I've already managed to get myself thrown out. Meek's words rang in my head as I made my way out of the classroom, Vaughn at my heels. *"You get one shot, Walsh."*

Well, I'd had my shot, and I'd blown it on the first day. I could almost hear the door of my prison cell sliding shut on my future with a metallic *clang*.

Chapter Three

We walked in silence all the way from the classroom to the Administrative Building where the teacher offices were, both of us lost in thought. Mine were on my future, or lack thereof. I'd sworn I would make a go of my stay of execution, get through the year at Stanton, and get my diploma. Maybe I would even go on to college, get a degree and a good job, move out of my dad's house. Now, all I had to look forward to was a year on the Juvie work farm, and that would be only if I was lucky. If not, my next address would be Cellblock B at the pen. I had no idea if the judge would seal my record after I was released, either, not after getting thrown out of school on Day One. It might haunt me for the rest of my days, and I couldn't help but think that my life, such as it was, was over.

Ambrosius' office was the third down on the left past Admissions. It was marked by a small brass plaque to the right of the door that read, "M. Ambrosius." The door was unlocked, and we let ourselves in.

The instant I entered the office, all of my worries were shocked right out of my head. For a moment, all I could do was stand still and stare.

The drapes hanging on the window behind Ambrosius' desk were open, flooding the room with light. The entire room—every inch of wall space, every shelf and tabletop, and most of the floor – was covered with odd bits and pieces of history. Swords, flags, statuettes, masks, pins, coins, scrolls, skulls, vases, and many items for which I had no name were on display. It was like walking into an extremely cluttered mini-museum.

"Wow. Where do you think he got all this stuff?" Vaughn asked, running a finger over a yellowed skull. It looked human but deformed. The forehead was sharply sloped and ended in a bulging brow. *H. neanderthalensis, Neolithic* was hand-printed in neat lettering on a small tag attached to the skull.

"I don't know," I answered with a shrug. I was too worried about my future to give a damn about where Ambrosius shopped for his old junk. "What do you think he's going to do to us?"

"*Us?* What us? You're the one who mouthed off. I just got caught up in the fall out. I'm out of here as soon as I can explain I had nothing to do with it," he sniffed.

"You agreed with me!" I argued.

"Did not. This is all your fault."

A sudden rush of anger clouded my vision. I was already stressed out knowing Principal Meek would welcome any excuse to throw me out because I'd screwed up my one chance at staying out of Juvie or worse, prison. Even if I'd done it to myself, I was looking for somebody else to blame, and Vaughn was in my direct line of fire. Plus, I was still a little jealous over his Rolex, matching luggage, and obvious money.

He'd agreed with me... we'd knuckle-bumped on it and everything. As far as I was concerned, he was just as much at fault for Ambrosius losing his temper as me.

Suddenly, my last nerve stretched too thin and snapped.

I reached out and gave him a little shove. "You're such a jerk off!" I yelled.

"Hey! Keep your hands off of me! Do you know who my father is?" He shoved back, rocking me on my feet.

"Jerk Off, Senior?" I snidely shot back, and gave him another poke. "Did he buy your girlfriend for you, too?"

"What are you talking about?"

"The chick sitting with you in court. She was your girlfriend, right? Did Daddy gift-wrap her for you, or is she a hand-me-down?" Mean, I know, but I was pretty angry, and when I got mad, my mouth tended to get verbal diarrhea.

His face turned beet red, and he launched himself at me, tackling me to the floor. A small, spindly table fell over with us. "That was my stepmom!"

Oh. Well... guess I read that one wrong, huh?

The Neanderthal skull fell, splintering into a dozen pieces. A plaster bust of some ancient Greek dude exploded into a shower of sharp shards and white dust.

We were so caught up in trying to beat the blame into one another that we barely noticed.

He banged my head on the floor, and I caught him in the ribs with an elbow. We rolled to one side, knocking over another table, and a rain of tiny, fossilized shells and teeth sprayed the floor. I was on top and popped him a good one in the jaw. I thought I had him until he heaved, and I suddenly found myself on the bottom. His fist connected with my mouth, and I saw stars.

My foot hit the wall, rattling several framed paintings hanging there. One fell off, hitting a shelf holding several Egyptian-looking jars with funky animal-head stoppers. They toppled, clinking together, and fell to the floor in pieces.

I pushed hard, and we rolled across the floor, taking out several more tables, until my shoulder hit the wall under the window. We twisted and scuffled, knocking over a delicate blue floor vase with golden dragons painted on it. It was full of fresh flowers, pale white blossoms that I had no name for. The vase cracked in half, and the water inside gushed out, flooding the floor. A good deal of it splashed the wall, dripping into the electrical outlet. Out of the corner of my eye, I caught sight of a brief spark and a curling wisp of smoke. Small flames began licking at the drapes hanging over the window. The curtains caught quickly, charring black as the fire ate its way through the heavy fabric.

The sight and smell of the fire were enough to break up our fight. We gasped and exchanged a terrified look. If we weren't in enough trouble before, we sure as heck were now. Vaughn grabbed a seat cushion from Ambrosius' chair and tried to beat out the flames, but it only made things worse. The cushion caught fire, too, and when he dropped it, the flames spread to the oval rug under his desk.

"Come on!" I yelled, grabbing his arm and tugging. The smoke was getting thick, and the fire was spreading. "We've got to get out of here!"

We fled the office into the hallway, slamming the door shut behind us as if it could contain the fire. There was no one in sight as I rushed to the opposite wall and broke the glass on the small red box labeled "In Case of Emergency." I hit the button inside, and a siren instantly began to wail.

Vaughn tugged frantically on my elbow. "Hurry up, before somebody sees us!"

I took one last look at the pitch-black smoke puffing

out from under Ambrosius' office door, then nodded and followed him outside.

We reached the Green just in time to hear the musical sound of glass breaking as the window of Ambrosius' office imploded from the heat. Smoke billowed outward in a thick, black column, and I could see tongues of flame licking at the exterior of the building.

As Vaughn and I ran, mixing in with the crowds of students pouring out from the campus buildings, alerted by the piercing fire alarm, I couldn't help but wonder what the jail time for arson was, and if anybody would ever believe it was all an accident.

Aside from a little scorching of the brick outside the building, the fire had been contained to the one room, but Ambrosius' office was completely destroyed. Nothing was left intact, not even a paper clip.

Speculation ran high as to the cause of the blaze. Some thought it was arson (I gulped and tried not to look guilty every time someone mentioned the word), some thought it was an electrical short, while other, less rational theories ran the gamut from poltergeists to freak lightning bolts.

Vaughn and I lived in a constant state of fear for four days solid. Neither of us slept, and we hardly ate. We were sure that they'd figure it out any minute, that someone would come forward and claim to have seen us entering Ambrosius' office, or running out of it at the time of the fire, or pulling the fire alarm. I was amazed that none of the teachers asked about my split lip or Grant's black eye. I guess everyone was too caught up in the aftermath of the fire to care much about a couple students sporting a few dents.

After all, Ambrosius knew he'd sent us there moments

before the fire. Why he hadn't had us dragged into Meek's office already was a mystery. Surely he must suspect that we had something to do with the fire! What was he waiting for? Was he so old and senile that he'd forgotten he'd sent us there?

No, I couldn't *possibly* be that lucky.

And, as it turned out, I wasn't.

Ambrosius hadn't been in class for three of those days—we'd had a substitute teacher. Presumably, he'd been going through the debris of what used to be his office, writing up reports for the insurance company on the artifacts he'd lost. I never questioned that they were worth beaucoup money. I doubted he'd picked them up at the local Walmart. As far as I knew, they were old, and might be priceless and irreplaceable.

On the fourth day, he was back in class. My heart jumped into my throat when I entered the classroom and saw the scowl on his face. His blue eyes blazed so fiercely they could've burnt holes into my skin.

He *knew*. He wasn't senile. He hadn't forgotten he'd sent us to his office. He *knew*.

I don't know to this day *how* I knew *he* knew we were guilty, other than the circumstantial evidence of knowing he'd sent us to his office minutes before, but I was as sure of it as I was of my own name. My knees were knocking as I made my way to my desk, and I could feel his eyes on the back of my neck. What was he going to do? Why hadn't he given us up to the police, yet? Or had he? Were they about to burst into the classroom and drag us off in handcuffs?

One look at Vaughn told me he was thinking the same thing. He was pale, and the hand that held his pencil shook.

"If you would please open your texts to page seventy, we will begin our study of Ancient Egypt," Ambrosius said. He gave no indication at all that today was going to be any different from any other day.

I sighed with relief, unaware I'd been holding my breath, and buried my nose gratefully in my textbook. Maybe I'd misread him. Maybe my own guilt was playing tricks on me. Maybe it wasn't anger at us that I saw burning in his eyes... maybe he'd just had a bad burrito for lunch.

And maybe birds are really fairy jet planes, piloted by pixies wearing tiny steampunk goggles.

The class went on without interruption. Time flew, and by the end of class, I had actually half-convinced myself that Vaughn and I were going to get away with it. I was so unsettled by what I regarded as my near-miss that I actually read along as one of the other kids read aloud. I even learned a few things and found myself interested in the history of the Ancient Egyptians in spite of myself, a first for me. I'd seen a documentary once on it, and remembered I'd thought it was pretty interesting.

Boy, was I wrong. Not about Egypt—about Ambrosius forgetting he'd sent us to his office.

"Mr. Walsh and Mr. Vaughn? Kindly remain after class. I need to speak with you both."

My stomach dropped into my sneakers as my fragile new hope died a swift but painful death. I was *so* screwed. He knew it was us all along and had just been playing with our heads, lulling us into a false sense of security. I was going to spend the next ten to twenty years of my life in the penitentiary with a cellmate named Bubba. I just knew it.

Vaughn and I exchanged a troubled glance and

remained in our seats as the rest of the class filed out of the room. A few tossed us looks of sympathy as they left, although I had to wonder if they knew the seriousness of our troubles. They probably just thought we hadn't done our homework or something. I could only wish it was something that trivial.

When the last student had gone, Ambrosius stood up and walked to the door, closing and locking it.

Locking it? My fear of being arrested was suddenly displaced by a new terror. What if Ambrosius was crazy and had decided killing us would be justified, since we'd destroyed his office and his collection? After all, he did keep an office bursting at the seams, full of old junk. Or used to, that is. How much was all that crap we burnt up worth, anyway? Thousands? Millions? People had been murdered for a lot less than that.

No, I told myself firmly, *don't be stupid. He's a teacher, not a serial killer. He's not going to pull a knife on you or anything.*

I hoped.

He walked toward us, the look on his face unreadable, but I was happy to see that he kept both of his hands in plain sight and, unless he planned on beating my head in with the blackboard eraser, there were no weapons anywhere that I could see.

"Gentlemen, as I'm sure you're well aware, we have a problem to discuss. I've pondered long and hard over it for the past couple of days, and I've come to a decision. Now, first things first... we all know who is responsible for the fire in my office, don't we?"

I instantly opened my mouth to deny my involvement, but Ambrosius held up his hand and the lie died on my tongue.

"Please, do not insult my intelligence by trying to convince me of your innocence. We, all three of us, know the truth. The problem we need to discuss is what I should do about it." His steely blue eyes looked from me to Vaughn and back again. "I *could* inform Principal Meek and the police that I sent you to my office just before the fire broke out. Such a course of action would no doubt result in your arrest, trial, and subsequent incarceration."

I felt the blood drain from my face, sure that my worst nightmare was coming true.

"Fortunately for you, I am aware that the fire was an accident. You were arguing, and your tempers got the best of you. That you did not purposely set the fire is the *only* reason I have not yet gone to the police."

"H-how did you know?" Vaughn asked, and I could've belted him a good one right there. He'd just admitted that, not only was Ambrosius right, that we'd been there, but that we'd been fighting and were the cause of the fire!

"I know many things, young man," Ambrosius answered, waving the question away. "How I come about my information is none of your concern." He perched on the edge of the desk in front of us and folded his hands. Those hands looked ancient; his skin was as thin as tracing paper, and I could see the squiggles of blue veins just beneath the surface. "I know you didn't mean to set the fire. Had you come to me straightaway, we would not be having this conversation. Accidents can and do happen, but you took the coward's way out, hoping no one would find out. You have both been in trouble with the law before, several times, from what I understand. You must learn that there is a price we must pay for our actions."

"I'm really sorry, Professor," I said. I saw Vaughn

nodding his head, and added, "We both are."

"Being sorry will not replace the artifacts I have lost, nor erase the possibility that someone might have been injured or killed in that fire. That said, since I do believe the damage was the result of an accident, I have decided to give you a choice."

"A choice?" I asked, exchanging a confused look with Vaughn. He didn't know where this was headed any more than I did.

"Yes. Accident or no, I must demand either restitution or justice. You can either agree to procure each and every item I lost in the fire, or you can go to jail and serve the sentence for whatever crime the authorities find you guilty of perpetrating."

Procure the items? I couldn't afford to buy a bar of soap, never mind any of the uber-expensive things Ambrosius had lost in the fire. Maybe Vaughn's family had enough cash on hand, but mine didn't. Heck, my dad was so fed up with me that, even if he *did* have the funds, I doubted he would have paid up.

"I don't have any money," I confessed. "My family doesn't, either. I guess I could get an after-school job." I tried to sound hopeful, but failed. If Ambrosius' collection was worth half of what I suspected, I'd never be able to earn enough to pay him back, not in one lifetime.

"Do you have any idea of the cost of the artifacts destroyed by the fire? They were irreplaceable. Priceless," Ambrosius said, scowling at me.

"But you just said one of our choices was to replace them!"

"No, I certainly did not. You weren't listening, Mr. Walsh, which I suspect is business as usual for you. What I *said* was that you could *procure* them. There's a distinct difference."

"I-I don't understand."

"Me, either," Vaughn put in. He'd been quiet up until then, and I wondered why. Surely Mr. Four-Names-And-A-Rolex's dad would be able to buy him out of this mess.

"It's quite simple, really. You will both go back in time to find and procure some of the items I've lost. Not all, since it would take many lifetimes to replace everything I lost, but some. Failure to do so will result in a telephone call to the police. The choice is yours, gentlemen."

"You're crazy!" I sputtered. "Back in time... what kind of a joke *is* this?"

"Oh, this is no joke, I assure you. Perhaps I should formally introduce myself. It might make things a bit more clear. You already know me by my surname, Ambrosius," he said, as a wicked little smile tilted his lips. "My first name is Merlin."

Then he waggled his fingers in the air as he whispered a few words in a language I didn't understand, and a thunderstorm broke. Lightning flashed and rain sluiced in sideways.

Inside the classroom.

Chapter Four

I don't know who moved faster—me or Vaughn. It was really too close to call. All I know is that one minute, we were sitting at our desks, and the next, we were flattened against the back wall, blinking rain out of our eyes.

It was definitely not a trick. He didn't hypnotize us. That much I knew straight off, as much as I wanted to believe otherwise. Magic tricks did not soak your hair and clothes with rainwater that fell from the perfectly dry ceiling tiles. Hypnosis made you bark like a dog or quack like a duck; it did not make the walls thrum with the volume of the crashing thunder, or send bright white zigzags of lightning sizzling through the air to disintegrate the world globe on Ambrosius' desk.

Then, when Mr. Ambrosius pointed at the destroyed globe and whispered another few words, the pieces jumped up and reassembled themselves seamlessly. That was something else that I figured would be impossible without the use of either Criss Angel or CGI effects.

Since this was real life and not a movie, and since I doubted Criss Angel made a habit of making guest appearances in high school history classes, I was leaning heavily toward believing Mr. Ambrosius was exactly who he said he was—Merlin.

King Arthur-Camelot-Sword-in-the-Stone-Excalibur-freaking-wizard *Merlin*.

Holy crap.

"W-what do you want from us?" I managed to stammer. My heart was banging against my chest so hard it was a wonder it didn't break clean through and go rolling across the floor.

"Haven't you been listening, boy?" Merlin asked. I could hear him plainly, even over the booming thunder and pounding rain. He flicked a finger toward the ceiling and the storm stopped, just that quick. An instant later, everything in the room was as dry as stale bread, including us—hair, skin, clothing, and all.

"You were serious?" Vaughn asked. "About sending us back in time? How are we supposed to do that?"

"I am never anything *but* serious, young man. Never mind the *how*; that is my concern. Yours is only to fetch back the artifacts you destroyed."

My head was spinning. On one hand, it was an exciting proposition, sort of the ultimate role-playing game. On the other hand, unlike RPGs, it was pure nuts. "*Time travel?* You honestly expect us to believe that you can send us back in time? Come on… that's crazy! I admit you put on a good show, with the rain and thunder and the globe and all, but…"

Merlin cocked one bushy white eyebrow. "Shall I call the police, then?"

"No!" Vaughn and I cried in unison.

"Good. Then we're agreed."

I exchanged another look with Vaughn. He seemed just as bewildered as I felt. Was it possible? Even if it was, did I really *want* to go back in time?

It could be kind of cool, I thought. Knights and

castles, merchants traveling in colorful, horse-driven caravans, Vikings rowing longboats, Roman charioteers, Wild West cowboys, and seeing the world as it was before computers, cars, and pollution...

On the other hand, there were diseases like the Black Plague, no inside plumbing, lots of sharp, pointy swords, and really short tempers.

On the *other*-other hand, think of what I could do in the past with the knowledge I had today! Imagine the people's amazement when I whipped out my MP3 player and made music float out of thin air, or taught them the secrets of the butane lighter! Heck, a bottle of Bayer aspirin would probably be enough to buy an entire kingdom.

I was excited for all of three minutes, until I reminded myself they used to burn people at the stake for using less "magic" than curing a headache with a little white pill.

"How are we supposed to even *find* the stuff you lost in the fire, never mind get it back even if we found it?" I asked.

Merlin smiled. "Ah, a pertinent question at last! You will know ahead of time what you are looking for, and when I send you back in time, I shall make certain to place you in the immediate vicinity of the item you are to procure for me."

"What are we supposed to do then?" Vaughn asked. "Steal the stuff?"

"Of course not!" Merlin looked highly offended by the suggestion that he was asking us to do anything illegal—even though, in essence, he was. "I did *own* the items, after all, until you destroyed them. The *exact* item, in fact. You are merely re-establishing ownership for me."

I blinked. That almost made sense, in a twisted,

convoluted sort of way.

Merlin pointed to me. "*You* stole an *automobile*. How much simpler would it be to retrieve a tiny brooch, or amulet, or other trinket?" He turned to Vaughn. "*You* broke into an office complex, despite the high security. How much easier would it be to enter a building *not* equipped with motion detectors and video cameras?"

Vaughn and I exchanged a meaningful look. We didn't say it out loud, but we were both thinking the same thing. Our pride wouldn't let us point out the one, glaring flaw in Merlin's logic.

Yes, I had stolen a car, and yes, Vaughn had broken into an office, but neither of us had *gotten away with it.*

We were thieves, I supposed, but not very good ones.

"What is your decision?" Merlin asked after a few moments of silence.

"I'll do it," Vaughn said.

I shot him a surprised look.

"What?" he asked, shrugging his shoulders. "I don't want to go to prison over a stupid mistake. Coming to this school was bad enough. Plus, we *owe* him. How would you feel if somebody destroyed all *your* stuff? At least he's giving us a chance to make it right."

Guilt, I realized, could do more to a guy's ethics than any lecture ever could. It was like the time when I was six and broke my mom's favorite lamp. It had been her grandmother's, and even as young as I was, I'd known it was special to her. I was scared I'd be punished, so I denied doing it. I told her everyone from a burglar to a leprechaun was responsible, but when she sighed softly and tears filled her eyes as she scooped up the broken bits of lamp, I cracked. I confessed because I felt so guilty at making my mom cry.

I figured it was the same sort of guilt that made Vaughn agree to Merlin's plan. I can't truthfully say I felt the same, although I did feel a surge of remorse because the fire really *had* been an accident. I hadn't liked Merlin for picking on me with the "Mr. Uh" stuff, but I hadn't wanted to destroy everything he owned because of it. That wasn't my style. In all honesty, though, it was the idea of being sentenced to the penitentiary for arson that decided it for me.

I had one more question. "How do we get back here again?"

"Once you have procured the item in question, I shall bring you back the same way I send you," Merlin said. It wasn't really an answer at all, but I could tell it was all I was getting out of him.

"But how will you know when we have the item?" Vaughn asked.

"Oh, I'll know. I have my ways," Merlin replied. Again, not an answer, but all we were likely to get. Merlin, it seemed, didn't like to share his trade secrets.

"Okay. I'll do it, too," I said. I shrugged. Anything was better than going to jail.

"Excellent!" Merlin said. He clapped his hands together like a big kid and smiled broadly. It was the first time I'd seen him smile since I started at Stanton, and I wasn't at all sure it was more comforting than the frown he usually wore. "It's best if we start immediately."

"Wait!" I said, afraid he was going to zap us into history that very minute. "Aren't people going to miss us here? Where are you going to tell them we've gone?"

"Time is foldable, Mr. Walsh. It expands and contracts, much like an accordion, and I have the power to play it perfectly. When you return from your jaunts to the past, I will refold it, and it will be as if only a few minutes have passed here."

Whoa. That was pretty heavy in a weird, Mr. Wizard kind of way. My mind struggled to wrap around the concept and failed. I decided it was easier to just take his word on it. Maybe that's why he didn't explain how he could do any of the stuff he did—it would be a waste of breath. He knew I'd never understand even if he did try to explain.

That made me a little angry. I was a juvenile delinquent, but I wasn't stupid.

Merlin went to the bookcase and pulled a fat volume from the shelf. He plunked it down on top of his desk with the cover facing Vaughn and me. There was a photograph of a golden face on it. It was a burial mask, and it looked familiar—I'd seen it before, on television.

King Tut, I recalled. *That's who it is.* The show I'd seen had been called "The Boy King," because Tut had been made king of Egypt when he was only eight or nine years old. I remembered thinking it was a pretty silly move to make a little kid king of an entire country. I mean, if the kiddie king misbehaved, who could give him a time out? He was the *king*, for corn's sake. You can't send the king to his bedroom for breaking curfew or not eating his vegetables.

They'd said on the show that Tut was only nineteen when he died, just a couple of years older than me. The narrator of the program had said Tut had been murdered. I'd supposed that any king, even a teenaged one, could be killed for his throne or the gold in his treasury. Nobody knew for sure who killed him, though. Some thought it was one of his advisors, a man named "Aye" or something, while others thought it might've been an assassin from one of the countries bordering Egypt. My money was on Aye. It was always the person closest to the murder victim, wasn't it? At least, it was in every movie I'd ever seen.

I remembered they'd said that Tut's tomb was discovered in the nineteen-twenties, and it had been filled with gold and treasure. Now, that had caught my attention! Imagine, digging a hole in the sand and finding gold and jewels and stuff! Was it finders-keepers? How awesome would that be?

I also remembered something about how, sometime after he died, Tut's name was erased from all the monuments and buildings and statutes. That seemed pretty harsh to me. I mean, after all the kid had been put through and being murdered so young and all, you'd think the least they could've done was to leave Tut's stuff alone. But no, it was like somebody going in and deleting your Facebook, MySpace, and Twitter accounts. If somebody Googled you, nothing would come up, as if you'd never existed at all! It was three thousand years before an archeologist named Carter discovered his tomb and people found out who Tut was.

The tomb was also cursed, or so they said. It was where Hollywood had gotten the idea for the *Mummy* movies. I'd thought that part was pretty cool, even if I didn't really believe in curses.

Then again, I hadn't believed in magic or time travel until about a half hour ago.

The title of the book on Merlin's desk was "The Wonders of Ancient Egypt." Merlin opened the book and flipped through the pages until he found the one he wanted. It was page two hundred forty-eight, and showed a picture of a piece of jewelry. It looked like a big, gaudy pin or pendant. According to the ruler lying next to the piece in the photo, it appeared to be about six inches long. The piece looked like it was made of gold, with colorful stones set into it. The black outline of a large eye was in the center, set above a pair of wings.

"This is an amulet once owned by King Tut, himself," Merlin said. "The eye you see in the center is called the 'Eye of Horus' or the 'Eye of Ra.' It was a very powerful symbol of protection. The ancient Egyptians thought it kept them safe from harm and ensured them good fortune. At other times, it was said to be linked to great destruction, to slaughter and death by fire."

I winced at the mention of 'fire,' the reason I was there in the first place.

"Your first task will be to retrieve this amulet. It was one of my most prized possessions," Merlin continued. "You will find yourselves in Memphis, a city on the Nile River. It was one of the cities where Tutankhamen lived and ruled during the time that is known as the New Kingdom. The amulet should be somewhere in his palace, most likely in his private quarters."

"How are we supposed to get into a king's bedroom?" I asked in disbelief. In my head, I pictured big, burly men dressed in white skirts and sandals, carrying huge, sharp scimitars, guarding the king's door. "Won't it be guarded? What are we supposed to do? Ring the bell and pretend we're selling magazine subscriptions for school?"

"The mechanics of gaining entrance is your problem," Merlin said. "I'm certain you two bright boys will figure it out."

Did I detect a trace of sarcasm in Merlin's voice? Of course I did. I looked at Vaughn and rolled my eyes. Adults, even ancient, magician adults, could be so lame!

"What about language?" Vaughn asked. "We don't speak Ancient Egyptian or whatever."

Good question. I wished I'd thought of it first.

"My magic will temporarily gift you with the ability to understand and speak whatever the local language is in whichever time and place you are. Sadly, language magic is short-lived. You will forget it the moment you return here, but it will suffice for your missions," Merlin explained. He made it seem so reasonable, as if using magic was an everyday occurrence, like making coffee or reading the paper. I guess, for Merlin, it was.

"Have you any more questions?" Merlin asked, looking first at me, then at Vaughn.

"No, I guess not," Vaughn said.

I wasn't quite done. I knew how these time-travel things worked. I'd watched enough movies and television.

"Is this were we get the 'don't change anything in the past' lecture that everybody gets in the movies where they go back in time? You know, the one that says if you kill a butterfly in the past, you'll come back to find everybody still living in caves or having three heads or something?"

Merlin snorted. "You *can't* change the past, young Mr. Uh, even if you try. Fate always finds a way to complete its master plan."

How was it that Merlin could make me feel like a complete idiot with one sentence every time I asked a question? Undaunted, I tried again. "What happens now?" I asked. "Do you need to make a potion in a cauldron with, like, eye of newt or tongue of frog to send us back?"

Merlin smirked at me. "Rubbish and nonsense. The magic is in *me*, boy, not in silly trinkets and props!" He closed his eyes and began murmuring in a strange language again, his long, bony fingers tracing patterns in the air.

I felt the floor under my feet tip, tilting like one of those platforms you'd find inside a funhouse at the county fair. I got dizzy and felt Vaughn grab on to my elbow, although I didn't know if it was because I was swaying or he was.

Suddenly, there was wind inside the classroom. It whipped our clothing and hair, and blew papers off Merlin's desk. It felt hot, like the wind at the beach in the middle of summer. It even *smelled* hot.

I glanced at Vaughn and realized with a start that I could nearly see through him. It was as if he were made of colored glass, almost transparent. I raised my hand in front of my face, and saw that I was disappearing, too.

My last thought before the entire universe imploded and stars so bright they hurt my eyes danced in my vision, the wind howling so loudly I couldn't hear anything else, not even my own screams, was that Merlin had better know what he was doing, or Vaughn and I were royally screwed.

Chapter Five

When I woke up, I was lying face down in hot sand. I could feel the broiling hot sun beating on my back, and my skin beginning to burn. For a split second, I thought I was on vacation with my dad and stepmom and had fallen asleep on the beach. I thought it was funny that I couldn't hear the ocean.

I sat up, and that's when I realized I wasn't at the shore. I was surrounded by smooth, golden, rolling hills of sand as far as I could see. The wind had whipped beautiful, abstract patterns in the sand like a sculptor carves stone.

Looking down, I realized my jeans and t-shirt had been replaced by a grayish, coarse linen skirt that fell to just above my knees. My tennis shoes had been swapped out with a pair of sandals that consisted of no more than a couple of stiff leather soles tied to my feet by rawhide thongs. I was wearing a hat... well, more of a headdress, really. It was white, tied around my forehead with a cord, and fell in soft folds to my shoulders. Hats were never really my thing, but since it was keeping the worst of the sun off my head, I kept it on. It hadn't occurred to me before that Merlin would dress us in the clothing style of the period, but it made sense. We'd never blend in wearing Levis and Nikes.

I looked to my right and saw Vaughn. He was lying on

his side, facing me, his eyes closed, dressed very similarly to me. I scooted over to him and shook his shoulder. "Hey! Hey, Vaughn! Wake up!"

His eyes cracked open, and for a minute I could see confusion in them. Then he must've remembered what had happened, and sat up so quickly he nearly knocked me over. "Where are we? Are we there? In Egypt?"

I gestured toward the sand surrounding us. "Either that, or he dumped us in the world's biggest kitty litter box."

"Funny," Grant said, in a tone that meant he didn't find me funny in the least.

Some people just don't have a sense of humor, I thought. "So, what do you think we should do now?"

He shrugged. "I don't know. Find the city Merlin mentioned, Memphis, and then find Tut's palace, I guess."

"Sounds like a plan," I replied. I jumped to my feet and extended my hand to help him up. After all, we were alone, just the two of us, and we were really, *really* far from home. We had only one another to depend on. Even though we hadn't been friendly before, I figured it would be best if we could be now.

He took my hand and gave me a smile, which I returned. Grant (since I wanted to be friends, I figured I should start calling him by his first name instead of his last) was a nice-looking guy, I realized, especially when he smiled. He had a little dimple in his cheek that you only saw when he grinned, and really pretty green eyes. I wondered why I hadn't noticed before.

Probably because I was too busy being jealous of his Rolex, four names, and private lawyer. Just goes to show what you can miss when you're busy being petty, I guess.

His hand was warm in mine, and I must have held it a

little longer than was necessary, because he pulled away from me with an odd expression on his face. I felt myself blush and turned away.

I liked boys. I always had, but maybe he didn't. *Probably didn't,* I told myself. *Don't be stupid and get all flirty with the guy. It'll make things even weirder than they are already.* I looked away and cleared my throat. "So, which way?"

Grant frowned as if deeply in thought, then brightened. "Assuming it's the same time here as it was when we left the classroom, then it's afternoon. And the sun is lower in that direction," Grant said, shielding his eyes as he looked up at the sky and pointed. "That means this way is west."

"Great. So... how do we know where the city is?"

He shrugged and grinned again. "I dunno. Sounded like I knew what I was talking about, though."

Giving him a playful shove, I laughed. "Yeah, you're a genius, all right. Listen, Merlin said he would stick us somewhere close to the object we need to find. Let's just climb one of the higher dunes and see if we can spot the city. It can't be far, unless Merlin botched it up."

"I hope not. If he did, we're really screwed. This is the Sahara desert. It's not like there's going to be a 7-Eleven or Walmart anywhere close by."

The image of an icy-cold, sixty-four ounce, 7-Eleven Coke Slushy suddenly exploded in my brain. I was thirsty. The sun was hot, and my mouth felt like I'd been chewing cotton balls. *Crap, just what I needed.* Why did he have to remind me that I was in a desert with nothing to drink? I plunged ahead, leading him across the sand as I wondered what passed for frozen, sugared beverages in ancient Egypt.

Climbing the dune was easier said than done. We had to continually shade our eyes with our hands or part of our headdresses to keep the windblown sand out of our eyes. Our feet slid on the soft sand, making walking difficult. Not to mention hot—imagine walking on a beach at noon. My feet felt like the skin was being baked right off my bones.

When we finally made it to the top, we both stopped and stared. Stretching out before us was a scene straight out of a history book. In the far distance, we could see three gleaming, white triangles, which I realized were the pyramids. They looked tiny from where I stood, but I knew the distance was playing tricks on my eyes—they were huge in real life, or so I'd heard. Closer was a bustling city full of people.

I don't really know what I expected to find when I got to ancient Egypt, but this wasn't it. I suppose I'd thought I'd see mud huts, maybe a crumbling pyramid, and everything would be really dirty, old, and cracked.

Memphis—if Merlin had gotten his magical On-Star right—was nothing like that. From what I could see from the top of the dune, it was beautiful. The buildings, walls, streets, and statues were white and clean. Gardens of flowers, trees, bushes, and ponds made bright splashes of color here and there.

Boats shaped like big, funky canoes dotted the Nile, the wide, blue-green river winding sluggishly alongside the reedy edge of the land. I caught sight of something slicing through the waters, and wondered if it was a crocodile. Maybe it was a hippo. I couldn't tell from that distance, but that was okay. I really didn't want to get up close and personal with either one of them.

I guess what startled me most was the *newness* of

everything, and the size of it all. Memphis wasn't a crumbling, small pile of ruins, like I'd imagined in my head. It stretched out along the banks of the Nile for a very long way. Nothing looked broken or destroyed. The buildings ranged from one-story huts to multiple-story houses. There were huge statues everywhere, some white and some painted with vivid colors. People moved along the wide streets, herding animals or carrying baskets. Others gathered at the riverbank, although I couldn't tell what they were doing. Getting water, maybe, or washing clothes or themselves. I could see children playing, waving ribbons, or chasing one another. The soft hum of a busy city drifted to us on the hot wind.

"Wow," Grant said. The awe in his voice matched what I was feeling exactly.

"Yeah. That's really something, huh?"

"Think it's Memphis?"

"It must be. At least, I hope so." I pointed toward the center of the city. "I wonder if that big building back there could be Tut's palace? I would think he'd be holed up in the biggest house in the city. If I were a king, that's where I'd hang my crown. Come on. Let's go down there and take a look," I said.

Going downhill was a lot easier and faster than going up had been. Gravity helped push us along. We started walking slowly down the steep slope of soft sand, but were soon running, our momentum carrying us, and we reached the bottom in a very short time.

We were at the edge of the city. A high wall surrounded Memphis, with openings cut at regular intervals. The closest opening to us was flanked by a pair of statues. They had the heads of men but the bodies of lions. They looked like the gigantic Sphinx I'd seen in the documentary about

Tut on television, but were much, much smaller. Even so, they towered over Grant and me. I didn't know if they were gods or kings, but they were impressive either way. Their painted eyes seemed to stare right at me, as if they knew I didn't belong there.

Freaky, I thought. *They give me the creeps.* I wouldn't say it out loud, of course. I didn't want Grant to think I was a wimp, getting spooked by a couple of statues. I pointed toward the river. "Maybe we should start there. We might be able to blend in with those people and follow them back into the city."

Grant nodded. "Good idea. Two strangers walking in through the front gates might draw too much attention."

It occurred to me that we were getting along, agreeing. I wondered about it for a while as we walked toward the river. Just like us and the ancient Egyptians, Grant and I were from two different worlds. My dad was working class, Middle America right down to his Elks Club pin and riding lawn mower. Grant's father was corporate America, with limousines and platinum credit cards. *My* dad had a bowling trophy. *His* dad had a trophy *wife.* We had nothing in common except for our rap sheets.

Yet here we were, thrown into a situation beyond the realm of either of our experiences, and we were getting along fine. Joking, laughing, just like we were friends.

Weird.

"What?" Grant asked me when we paused behind a shielding screen of ferns. On the other side, people waded in the shallows of the river, scooping out urns of water and washing clothes. Little kids screamed and splashed nearby. There were several men with long, wicked-looking pikes standing guard, although whether against strangers like us or crocodiles, I didn't know. I was hoping for the crocs.

"What, *what*?" I asked.

"You were staring at me."

"Sorry. My mind wandered." Yeah, it *had*, too, all over the fact that he was shirtless, and had a pretty decent body, and a perfect tan. *Back off, Walsh,* I told myself. *No flirting, remember? Focus.* "Are you ready?"

"Yeah, let's do this thing," Grant replied. He gave me a small, shaky grin and nodded.

We each took a deep breath and stepped out of the reeds.

Chapter Six

To our relief, we attracted nothing but a few curious glances. Perhaps strangers were a commonplace sight in Memphis. It made sense if the king made his home there, that dignitaries and other visitors would come to the city. I only hoped nobody would try to talk to us. Even though Merlin had promised we'd be able to speak in the language of whatever time period and country we were in, I was hesitant to try it out. What if I struck up a conversation with an ancient Egyptian, only to find out I was speaking Swahili or Chinese?

Grant and I moved through the crowd, trying to keep our heads low and not make eye contact with anyone as we headed toward the steady stream of people walking back and forth from the shore of the Nile to the city gates.

We passed by another set of the stone sphinxes I'd seen earlier, and entered a spacious, square marketplace. Colorful booths lined the square, selling everything from bolts of cloth to pungent spices and jewelry. Merchants called out to us as we passed, jingling bracelets and necklaces, waving peacock or ostrich feathers, or holding up squawking chickens, trying to entice us to their booth.

The one good thing I realized immediately was that I could understand them! Merlin had kept his word about the language magic.

"Young master, come see! I have Nubian gold, very nice! Come see!"

"My wares are the rarest in all of Egypt! Come see my cloth, the best linen made only from the finest flax!"

"Furs! Fox and hyena! Come see my fine furs!"

"Barley! Wheat! Sesame seeds, and honey, here! Come, a taste for the young master!"

My stomach rumbled at the sweet smells coming from that last booth. I nudged Grant and nodded in the direction of the merchant. "Come on," I whispered. "Free samples!"

"We need to find Tut," Grant said. "We don't have time to sightsee."

"Yeah, well, we're not going to be able to sneak into the palace if my stomach is growling like a bear, either. We missed lunch, remember? Come on, it'll only take a minute," I insisted. I hurried over to the merchant.

"What shall it be, young master?" The merchant was an older man with skin like leather. One eye was milky-blue and stared straight ahead. The other was nut-brown and shrewd.

"Um, that bread. What kind is it?" I asked. It was really strange to hear myself speak in ancient Egyptian. I didn't have to try to think in Egyptian, either. I just spoke the way I always did, in English, but my lips formed words that I'd never heard before. My ears heard a fluid stream of nonsense syllables, but my brain understood every word spoken. It was disconcerting, but I figured I'd get used to it. I'd have to, if I was going to retrieve all of Merlin's lost artifacts.

"It is honey-wheat, young master. A taste, perhaps?" He broke off a small piece and handed it to me.

This was not the sliced white bread I was used to! The

texture was rough and grainy, with whole seeds stuck inside the dough, and there was a hint of sweetness to it, probably from the honey. It wasn't bad, though, just not what I was used to. I ate it and nodded. "It's good," I said.

"How many loaves do you wish, young master? One piece of brass will buy five loaves. It is a bargain, yes?"

I didn't want to tell him that I didn't have any money. Who knew if there was a penalty for taking free samples if you had no money to buy the goods you liked? "I'm in a hurry now, but I'll come back later," I said, and left. The merchant yelled angrily at my back. I glanced over my shoulder and saw him shaking his fist at me. I guess he'd expected to make a sale since I obviously had liked the bread, but all I'd done was eat his merchandise and leave. I suppose he felt gypped.

"Nice. We're here five minutes and you've already pissed somebody off," Grant grumbled when I caught up with him.

"I couldn't help it. I was hungry. I figured it was like when you go the grocery store and somebody's handing out free samples. Nobody expects you to buy the stuff right away."

"Evidently, they do here. No more samples, okay? If we get arrested, we'll never be able to get Merlin's amulet, and we'll never get home again."

I nodded. At least my stomach had quieted—for now. That little bit of bread wasn't going to stave off starvation for long, not when I'd been known to pack away a couple of quarter-pound cheeseburgers, fries, and a shake without barely pausing to swallow.

As we made our way toward the gleaming building I'd thought might be Tut's palace, I began to notice a few things about the Ancient Egyptians.

First, they all wore makeup. From the oldest to the youngest, they'd painted their eyelids with dark gray or green color that extended past the outer corner of the eye in a straight line. Some had reddened their cheeks and lips, too, and most had colored their fingernails orange or yellow.

Weird.

"What's with the makeup?" Grant asked in a whisper.

"Beats me."

"It looks like a drag queen competition."

Wow. I wouldn't have thought Grant knew what a drag queen *was*, let alone that they had beauty pageants. It was food for thought, but for later. I had more pressing things to think about now, like how I was supposed to steal an amulet out from under the nose of King Tut.

The second thing I noticed was that, in Memphis, clothing was optional. Little kids wore nothing but their skins, and while some women wore sleeveless dresses, most people only wore skirts. Few people wore even sandals. No one batted an eye at all the nudity, either. I guess they were used to seeing everyone else's bits and pieces, and they didn't care.

It was a little embarrassing for me, though. I felt like a skeevy Peeping Tom, and I know my cheeks were red, which only made me more uncomfortable because I was trying hard to be cool and pretend that I'd seen it all before, but I knew that one look at my blotchy face surely gave me away. I didn't mention it to Grant, but I figured I didn't need to point out the obvious. His cheeks were sort of rosy, too.

Luckily, the building we thought might be Tut's palace was just ahead. It gleamed bright white under the desert sun. The entire front of the building was such a mass of sculptures, hieroglyphics, and paintings that I didn't know where to look first.

We ducked into the slightly cooler shadows cast by the magnificent building, watching, trying to figure out how to get inside. Didn't a person need a special invitation to enter the palace of the king? I didn't think the average Joe Schmuck could just waltz inside whenever he felt like it.

It seemed I was wrong. As we watched, a steady parade of people entered the palace. *The king must be a pretty busy guy if he gets that much business every day*, I thought, watching what seemed to be an endless line of people disappearing inside the beautiful building. There were guards armed with curved swords, but they didn't seem overly concerned with who was waiting to enter, so Grant and I slipped into the line.

We kept our heads down as we passed the guards. I expected a big hand to clamp down on my shoulder, demanding to know why I was trying to get inside the palace, but to my relief, none did. We passed through the immense, golden double doors easily.

Grant and I found ourselves at the tail end of a traffic jam. It was very hot, and I wiped sweat out of my eyes. I supposed all the body heat crammed inside the hallway was raising the temperature even higher than it already was. People filled the wide, long corridor from side to side and end to end, and no one seemed to be going anywhere. Craning my neck, I could see another set of golden doors far ahead. People were being let in two and three at a time.

It was then that I noticed that everyone seemed to be carrying something—carved boxes full of large gold rings, armfuls of ostrich and peacock feathers, food, or bolts of cloth. Four men carried a cage in which a cheetah paced, its long tail swishing back and forth. Another man had a gigantic, bright yellow boa constrictor wrapped around his body.

Was everyone supposed to bring a gift when they came to the palace? I felt kind of like a kid showing up at a birthday party without a present. *Tut must be spoiled rotten,* I thought peevishly, *if all he does all day is get gifts. What a life!* I was lucky if I got a video game or a pair of jeans at Christmas and on my birthday, and here Tut was, getting gold and live animals and stuff. It just wasn't fair.

Grant grabbed my elbow and nodded toward the left. There was another, smaller hallway branching off from the main one. With a quick glance at the guards to make sure they weren't looking (they were busy with the men carrying the cheetah, which was snarling and trying to slip a paw tipped with razor-sharp claws through the bars of its cage) we slipped out of the crowd and down the second passageway.

There was no one around. We both breathed a sigh of relief to be out of the crowd and away from the guards. Now all we had to do was find Tut's bedroom, where we figured the amulet would be.

Our leather sandals made soft clicking noises against the marble floor as we walked. The hallway was much shorter than the main one, and led into a square, lush garden surrounded by high white walls and open to the sky.

Flowering bushes and trees filled the garden. There was a small, clear pool at its center. Wading in water up to his knees was a guy about our own age. Like everyone else in Memphis, he was wearing only a skirt, except his was intricately pleated and trimmed in gold. His head was clean-shaven except for a few long braids that began on the top of his skull and hung down past his shoulders, tied with colorful beads. His skin was the color of burnished copper, and he had a nice, if slender, build.

He turned and stared at us. His eyes were very dark, almost black, and outlined in dark green makeup. He was a good-looking guy, almost too pretty, with delicate features and a slightly receding chin.

And he was wearing Merlin's amulet. He had to be King Tut, himself!

Chapter Seven

"Who are you? What are you doing in my gardens?" Tut demanded. He was frowning, and I could tell he wasn't pleased at all to find two strangers gawking at him in his private garden.

"Uh, we're sorry, your, uh, your...," I stammered. How did you address a king? I couldn't remember if it was My Lord, Your Highness, or Your Majesty. I tried to think of what kings were called in video games. "My Liege."

Tut's frown intensified, and I realized I must've picked the wrong title. Damn it, why didn't Merlin give us a clue before we left? Then again, I suppose he was hoping we'd get in and get out with the amulet without ever running into Tut. Yeah, and if wishes were fishes we'd be up to our nose hairs in tuna.

Luckily, Grant took Tut's attention away from me by executing a deep bow. "Forsooth, Ye Majesty, we humbly beg thy forgiveness! We have strayed from the path and wandered by error into thy presence." He actually tried to fake a British accent.

He failed, and sounded like Monty Python on helium.

I turned and smacked him on the arm. "Where do you think you are? In the middle of *Macbeth*? They don't talk like that here."

He turned on me with a scowl, rubbing his arm. "How

do you know what they sounded like? When were *you* here last? Wait, let me think… oh, that's right. *Never*! At least *I* got out a full sentence!"

"I was working on it!"

"Yeah, well, you weren't working fast enough. He would've thought we were idiots!"

"And he would've been *half* right," I huffed.

Grant snarled and gave me a push.

I pushed back, a little harder than I'd intended. He rocked on his feet, losing his balance, but before he fell over onto his butt into the small pond with a big splash, he managed to grab my arm and drag me in with him.

It wasn't that deep, but I fell backward and my head went under. I came up sputtering and seeing red, but my anger paled quickly. I was horrified to see that we'd managed to knock Tut over, too! He was sitting in the pond, sopping wet. There was a leaf plastered to his skull.

Oh, man. We'd blown it big time. Tut was going to yell for his guards any second now!

To my amazement, Tut didn't call for the men with the sharp, curvy swords.

Instead, he laughed.

I mean *really* laughed. He threw his head back and laughed so hard that tears came to his eyes, smudging his makeup, and he snorted.

He sounded just like any other kid, laughing at something stupid his friends had done. Grant and I exchanged a dumbfounded look, then started to chuckle, too. I suppose we couldn't help it. It wasn't every day that you found yourself sitting next to one of the most famous dead people in the world, up to your armpits in pond scum.

"Sorry, Tut," I said, struggling to my feet. I held out a

hand to help him up out of the water.

"*Tut?*" He seemed to find that funny, too, and laughed again. "My name is Tutankhamen. How is it that you don't know my name? Everyone else does. Sometimes I tire of hearing it." He affected a high-pitched falsetto. "*Tutankhamen*, come here. *Tutankhamen*, go there. *Tutankhamen*, do not get your kilt dirty. *Tutankhamen*, it is time for your appointment with your tutor." He rolled his eyes. "My second-mother, Nefertiti, never leaves me a moment's peace."

I grinned. I knew exactly how he felt. "Sounds like my stepmom. I'm Aston, and this is Grant."

Grant smiled at him and gave a little half-wave.

"Strange names," Tut said. "I have not heard such before. You must not be Egyptian. From where do you come?"

"The U.S.," I answered.

He cocked his head. "You-Ess? I have never heard of such a place. Who is your king?"

"It's really far away. We don't have kings. We have presidents," Grant said.

Tut laughed again. "You are very funny. Everyone has a king." He stepped out of the pond and reached for a piece of linen, wiping his face. His makeup came off, but he didn't seem concerned about it. I supposed he had somebody ready to redo it if he needed it. A personal assistant or something. Most rich people had them, I guessed. Without his eyeliner, he looked even more like an average teenager. "Now, what is the name of yours?"

"Kong," I said, wincing as the first name I thought of slipped out of my mouth. "King Kong." I heard Grant swear softly under his breath, but Tut didn't bat an eye.

Tut shrugged. "I have not heard of him. But then,

there are too many places with too many kings, are there not? Even we once had two, until my ancestor, Menes, may he live forever, united Upper and Lower Egypt." He bent and used the linen to wipe his feet. "So, why have you come to Egypt? Has your King Kong sent you with tribute?"

I couldn't tell him we were there to steal his amulet, but I didn't have anything to give him, either. If I'd been wearing my jeans, I probably would've found something—a key, or stick of bubble gum, *something*—but kilts didn't have pockets.

He waved a hand at me. "Never mind. That was a silly question. *Everyone* sends tribute, because *everyone* wants Egyptian gold. Did you know the king of Mesopotamia once told my grandfather he believed gold was like dust here? He must've been a very stupid man to think such a thing. Our gold comes from the mines in Nubia," Tut said. Then he changed the subject as swiftly as the wind changes direction. "I am hungry. You will eat with me. The cook has made duck, and it is my favorite." He turned and walked away, as if fully expecting us to follow him. He didn't seem to care that he was dripping water all over the floors of the palace as he headed down a corridor.

Of course, we followed him. After all, it didn't seem wise to turn down an invitation to lunch with the king. Plus, my stomach was starting to growl again. I'd never had duck before, but I figured I was hungry enough to chew rocks. We followed several paces behind him, dripping, too.

"Did you see it?" Grant asked me in a whisper.

"The amulet? Yes," I answered, nodding. "How are we supposed to get it if he's wearing it?"

Grant shrugged. "We'll have to wait until he takes it off."

"What if he never takes it off? What if it's like a lucky charm or something?"

Grant didn't have a chance to answer me because at that moment Tut looked over his shoulder at us and told us to hurry along. He looked impatient. We stopped talking and walked faster, since we certainly didn't want him to overhear us plotting to steal his jewelry. We'd never get the amulet *or* lunch if he had our heads chopped off.

Not that Tut seemed the type of guy to do such a thing, but you really never knew, right?

He led us up a steep flight of stairs that were made from carved blocks of stone, and down another hallway. I thought we'd been heading to a dining room or kitchen, but the room Tut eventually brought us into didn't have a table. Instead, it had a low, wide bed covered head to foot in overstuffed pillows and embroidered linens. Several ornately carved wooden boxes and chests were scattered around. Woven rugs in bright colors covered the floor. There was a big, glassless window in the room, and I realized it overlooked the same garden where we'd met. Was it his bedroom? From the looks of the big bed, I figured it was.

Tut sat on the wide bed and motioned for us to join him. Servants appeared seemingly out of nowhere, rushing to fluff Tut's pillows and make him comfortable. One stood at his side with a handful of black and white ostrich feathers tied to a long stick, slowly fanning him.

Another servant took up a station near the door and tasted a bit of each dish brought in before it was offered to Tut. I realized the servant was testing the food for poison. *Jeez*. And here I thought I had it bad because I was paranoid about my stepmom going through the dresser drawers in my room when I wasn't at home! I couldn't imagine being worried that somebody would poison my bologna sandwich!

It also reminded me that Tut would be murdered in a couple of years. Logically, I knew that by the time I was born he would've been already dead for three millennia, but somehow, as he sat next to me picking a seed out of his teeth, it seemed even more... *final*. How could this very much alive boy be the same one who would be found mummified by archeologists in the 1920s?

Then I remembered what that documentary had said about the mummification process, and I completely lost my appetite.

First, they cut you open and ripped out your lungs, liver, stomach, and intestines. The only thing they left in place was the heart. Then they shoved a long hook up your nose into your brain. It was like the hook was the ancient Egyptian version of a blender set on puree, and they were making a brain smoothee. Then they pulled the whole mess out through your nose and threw it away. The rest of your organs went into little bottles called "canopic jars," which they buried with you. Then they'd stuff what was left of your body with salt and leave you to dry out for forty days! By the time they were ready to wrap you with one hundred and fifty yards of linen, you looked like a dried-out corn husk.

I couldn't imagine them doing that to Tut. He'd only been nineteen! I sure as shooting wouldn't want to be turned into a mummy before I was old enough to have a beer or rent a car.

An idea dawned on me. Maybe it didn't have to happen that way. If I warned Tut that someone was out to murder him, he could protect himself, right? I didn't give a flying rat's butt about Fate, or whatever Merlin said about changing the past. I promised myself I would find a way to make sure Tut lived. After all, I reasoned, it was the least I could do, considering I was going to steal his amulet.

Feeling much better, I dug into the platters now heaped around us. There was bread, of course, except this had a much finer texture than the bread I'd tasted in the market place. It still wasn't the white, sliced bread I was used to, not by any stretch of the imagination, but it tasted good. It was more like the coarser whole-grains bread my health-conscious stepmother bought from the specialty foods store.

Besides the bread, there were green olives, figs, dates, and roasted meat, all washed down with a cup of sweet wine. I grinned at Grant when I realized there was wine in my cup. My drinking *any* type of alcohol would've freaked my dad out, but I couldn't risk offending Tut by not drinking his wine, now could I? We ate with our fingers, and licked them clean afterward.

"Tell me about this place you are from," Tut said after we'd finished eating. He leaned back on his elbows, his dark eyes watching me. "What was the name? You-Ess? It must be a very insignificant country if I have not heard of it."

Okay, king or no king, I wasn't going to let Tut knock the good ol' U.S. of A. "It's called the United States, U.S. for short, and it's not insignificant. It's five or six times bigger than Egypt!" I snapped, sticking out my chin. I might've been a thief, and a "C" student at best, but nobody could say I wasn't patriotic.

Tut laughed at me. "You are a funny man. No country is bigger than Egypt! Egypt is the greatest country in the world! I thought everyone knew this."

Grant flicked me on the back of the head with two fingers. "Of *course* we know Egypt is the greatest country in the world," he said. The warning was clear in his voice. I could almost hear him saying, "Don't go upsetting the king, not until after we get the amulet!"

"Do you have hippopotamuses in this You Ess?" Tut asked. "Their meat is good. We hold it sacred and only eat it on special days. Their tusks are useful, and our artisans carve them, but the animal is very dangerous to hunt. They kill many of our people every year. The only good hippopotamus is a roasted hippopotamus," he said wryly.

"No, no hippopotamuses," I said.

"Crocodiles?"

"No."

"Gazelles?"

"No."

Tut raised an eyebrow. "No gazelles? They are good eating. No matter. I will send some home with you when you return."

I bit back a laugh, picturing us showing up in Merlin's classroom with a couple of slender, long-horned gazelles in tow. Then the laugh escaped me as I thought of the expression on Dean Meek's face if he saw them. "That's very generous of you, Tut."

"*Tutankhamen,*" he said. "Can you not remember my name?" He turned to Grant, but gestured toward me. "Is he simple minded?"

"Yes," Grant said with a completely straight face. "Very."

I socked him one on the arm for that. "I'm not stupid. Where we come from, friends sometimes use nicknames—

shorter versions of their full names."

"Ah, a You-Ess custom. I see," Tut said. He looked thoughtful for a moment, then added, "Ass."

Ass. Short for Aston, I realized. Great. First it was "Mr. Uh," and now it was "Ass." My nicknames were really starting to suck.

Grant thought this was uproariously funny. Did I mention that he could be a real jerk sometimes? "So, *Ass*," he said, "Why don't you ask Tutankhamen about his necklace? I noticed you were admiring it earlier."

Make that a complete and utter jerk off.

"Uh, yeah. It's... really pretty," I said lamely. "What is it?"

Tut looked down, lifting the beautiful gold amulet in his hand. "It is a charm against evil. As long as I wear this, I have the protection of Ra," he said, pointing to the eye in the center of the amulet. "He watches over me."

"It looks pretty heavy," I added. I knew from Merlin that Tut's amulet was solid gold and studded with large pieces of turquoise, lapis, amethyst, and malachite.

Tut shrugged. "I am used to its weight. I have worn it since I was very young. I only take it off when I sleep and bathe."

Well, crap. Unless we were going to hit Tut over the head and snatch the necklace from around his neck, we'd have to wait until he fell asleep! I didn't want to hurt Tut. He was cool, in a slightly overbearing, I'm-the-king-and-you're-not sort of way. It looked like we were going to be in ancient Egypt longer than I'd anticipated. I'd thought we'd only be there for a few hours at most. Plus, I was still determined to make sure Tut didn't end up on the ancient Egyptian equivalent of a milk carton.

I looked at Grant. He seemed to be thinking the same

things I was, and didn't look any happier about it than me. How long were we going to have to stay in Egypt?

Chapter Eight

"You have not told me what brings you to Egypt," Tut said. His dark eyes flickered back and forth from Grant to me.

"Uh, yeah, about that... we..." Grant began, but looked at me to finish.

Coward. Well, I already said he could be a jerk, didn't I?

"We heard so much about Egypt," I lied. "You know, about the Great Pyramids and the Sphinx and all. We wanted to see it for ourselves."

I guess it was a good answer, because Tut smiled and nodded. "The tombs of my ancestors are indeed a grand vision. Did you know it took over twenty thousand men eighty years to build the tomb of Khufu, the largest of them?"

"Wow, that's a lot of manpower," I said, meaning it. Twenty *thousand* men? That was like an entire town full of people! And they kept at it every day for eighty *years*? Some people didn't even *live* that long, especially back in ancient times! It blew my mind to think of all of those people living and dying, generations of them, putting up block after tremendous stone block, day after day.

"I have not visited the tomb of Khufu to leave an offering for a long time. On the morrow we will go, and you will see the artistry of my people for yourselves," Tut said. It was obvious that he didn't think we'd disagree with him. "You will take back tales of our skill to your You-Ess."

Leave an offering? I swallowed hard and hoped the offering Tut had in mind wasn't human. I knew the Aztecs sometimes sacrificed people to the gods. Did the Egyptians do the same? "Uh, sure, that'd be great, Tut."

"You will spend the night here, in my palace," Tut said. He clapped his hands together twice. A servant hurried to his side. "Take my new friends to a chamber so that they might rest. See to it they are bathed and perfumed, and treated as valued guests of Egypt."

Oh, no. Not perfume! I didn't even like to wear cologne. And I hadn't needed anybody to wash me since I was five years old! A quick glance told me Grant didn't look any more enthusiastic than I felt.

Plus, if we were in another room, how would we be able to steal the amulet? Things were not going as we'd planned, not at all, but there didn't seem any way for us to get out of it, not without offending Tut. I was still mindful of the big men outside the door to Tut's bedroom, the ones with the big, sharp, curvy swords.

"Thanks, Tut," Grant said. I echoed him, meaning it about as much as he did.

"I will see you on the morrow, with the rising of the sun. It is not an over-long journey to the tombs, but I wish to be there before the worst heat of the day. Sleep well, Grant and Ass." Tut stood up, and his servants immediately began readying his own bath. When they stripped off his kilt, I figured we were dismissed and it was time for us to leave.

We followed Tut's servant to another room, farther

down the hall from Tut's. It wasn't as big as Tut's room. The bed was smaller, laid with white linen and a few pillows, and there were only a couple of rugs on the floor. It was still a nice room, though, and bigger than my bedroom at home. My favorite piece of furniture was a table shaped like a cheetah. The cheetah's back was long and flat and held a bowl of water with flower petals floating in it. Kind of girly, but it smelled nice. A few fat white candles burned next to the bowl. Torches flickered in wall sconces. They were the room's only source of lighting.

I sat on the bed and looked up at Grant. "So, what do we do now?"

"Wait until Tut falls asleep, then sneak into his room and take the amulet?"

"Brilliant. Except I doubt those big guards of his sleep while on duty. How do you figure we get past them?"

"Good point. Maybe you can distract them while I go inside to get the amulet."

"If you what you mean by 'distract them' is letting them chop me up into Aston Sushi, then I'll have to pass. Try again, Einstein."

Grant huffed and folded his arms across his chest. "Well, I don't hear any ideas coming from your corner, *Ass*. What do *you* think we should do?"

I cringed at his use of Tut's nickname for me. "If I knew, I wouldn't have asked *you*." I lay back on the pillows, staring at the ceiling. "I guess we're going to have to wait. Maybe we can snatch it on the trip to the pyramids."

Grant looked panic-stricken. His face was pale in the dim candlelight as he began to pace back and forth in front of the bed. "We can't go sightseeing! We have to get back to the school. We can't stay here forever!"

"Calm down. We won't. Another day won't matter. Remember what Merlin said about time? We could stay here for a year, and only a few minutes will probably have passed back home." I didn't know if it was true, but I sure hoped it was. I figured we didn't have any choice but to trust Merlin on that one.

He calmed down a little—or at least, he stopped pacing. "Yeah, I remember. I still don't want to stay here one minute longer than we have to."

"And you think I *do*? No television. No video games. No cell phones. No air conditioning. There aren't even any bathrooms!" Mentioning that last one made me aware of the fact that I had to go, something I'd been studiously trying to ignore for the past few hours. I felt like an overfilled water balloon about to pop. "What do you suppose they use for toilets, anyway?"

Grant shrugged. "I don't know. A pot?" He gestured toward a tall earthenware vase on the floor. It was painted with Egyptian figures, and reached past my waist. I figured I'd need to stand on the bed in order to make the shot neatly.

"Maybe I should just pee out of the window," I said, eyeing the tall pot and shaking my head doubtfully.

That finally brought a smile to Grant's face. "I can just imagine people looking up at the sky and wondering where the yellow rain was coming from. I just hope you don't have to do anything else."

I wrinkled my nose, but couldn't help laughing, too. "Gross!" Still and all, when you have to go, you have to go. I poked my head out of the window and looked down, just to make sure no one was standing underneath it, then let it fly.

My business had just finished when a handful of women entered our room. Evidently, ancient Egyptians didn't knock on doors. They just walked on in. I thought it was a good thing I wasn't in the middle of showering the streets of Memphis with golden rain, because I might've fallen right out of the window.

I wondered briefly whether if I died in the past if I'd be instantly transported to the present, and if I'd still be dead when I got there. I sure as heck didn't want to find out the answer.

The women, wearing long, plain white, sleeveless dresses and carrying big vases, went directly to a low, square tub I hadn't noticed before, and poured water into it. They left, and more women came in, all silent and all carrying jugs of water that were poured into the tub.

Finally, two more women came in and stood expectantly at the side of the tub. They were older than us, although not by much. After a few minutes of mutual staring with neither Grant and me or them speaking, one of them broke the stalemate by asking, "Young masters will bathe now?"

No. Oh, *hell* no. I didn't even like to shower with the other guys after gym class. There was no way I was getting naked with these strange women in the room! Not to mention seeing Grant naked, who I still thought was pretty hot, despite our current almost-friends relationship and my thoughts that he could be a jerk. Ever since I turned fifteen, my body had grown a mind of its own, and I knew exactly what would happen to me if I saw him without even that skimpy little kilt covering his essentials. Plus, if I was naked and in same tub, *he'd* see *me,* and that would just make everything worse.

"Uh, I think we're good," Grant said. His face

darkened, and I knew in the sunlight it would be bright red. I wondered for a moment if he was thinking along the same lines as me, but told myself to get a grip. He was straight, right? I mean, he'd never said he had a girlfriend or anything, but then, we hadn't known each other for very long before the whole Merlin-time-travel-disaster thing happened. Still, he'd never looked at me as if he was interested in anything but grabbing Merlin's artifact and getting home again.

The women looked confused. "Young masters bathe now, yes?"

"No," I said. "No bath, not tonight. We're really tired. We want to go to sleep."

"Yes, sleep," Grant agreed. "We'll take a bath tomorrow. At the river," he added. Mentioning the Nile was a stroke of genius, because the women nodded and left the room. Most of the ancient Egyptian people must bathe there regularly, I reasoned. Plus, it ensured that nobody would come barging in bright and early the next morning and try to get us into the tub.

We looked at each other and sighed after the women left, silently agreeing that we'd averted a near-major disaster. I knew what my reasons were, and was less than sure of his, but it was apparent we were equally happy with the outcome.

Dirty, but happy. A little smelly, but happy. I figured it was a small price to pay for my self-respect.

I was about to lie down and go to sleep when he pointed to a square, wooden box next to the tub. It had a hole cut in the center, and I knew as soon as he pointed it out that I hadn't had to shower the good people of Memphis with my body fluids after all. It was an ancient Egyptian potty.

Swell.

I lay down and rolled my back to him as Grant made use of the facilities, such as they were. By the time he was finished, I must have been drifting off to sleep, because I never felt him crawl into bed.

When I dreamed, it was of a bronze-skinned young man in a kilt, but I couldn't decide if it was Tut or Grant.

I wished I knew which one it was, because in my dreams, I kissed him.

And he liked it.

Chapter Nine

We awoke the next morning with the sun streaming in through the window of our room and a loud commotion echoing in the halls outside of our door.

People were shouting, and we could hear feet running back and forth, bare soles and sandals slapping the marble floor. We sat bolt upright in bed, looking at each other. Had we been discovered? Did Tut and his people somehow learn that we were there to steal the amulet?

My heart was pounding. We each quickly took care of the necessities, one turning his back politely as the other did his business, but we talked nonstop during the entire process.

"Do you think they know?" I asked in a whisper. I was facing the far wall, keeping my back turned toward Grant.

"How could they?" Grant replied from behind me. "It's not like they saw our pictures on the news or hung up in a post office. Besides, if they knew about us, they'd be in here dragging our butts out to Tut by now."

"Then what's going on out there?" I looked down and was surprised to find a pair of twig-like brushes next to a bowl of water on the cheetah table. It took me a minute to figure out it was the ancient Egyptian version of a toothbrush. I smiled gratefully and used one to scrub the sleep-scum from my teeth while I waited for Grant to finish.

"I don't know. I was in here with you, remember?" He was next to me now, tugging on my arm. "Come on. We have to go out there and try to figure out what's happened."

He made sense, and I nodded, following him to the door.

We cracked open the door and peeked outside. Servants were running up and down the halls, and all of them had worry etched into their expressions. Something was wrong, all right, and it was something bad, from the look of fear in the servants' eyes.

I reached out and grabbed a boy's arm, pulling him to a halt. "What's happened?"

He turned wide, kohl-lined eyes at me. "The queen mother is missing! Ra protect us! Osiris guard us!" He jerked away from me and ran off.

"Tut's mother? Nefertiti?" Grant asked.

Something about Nefertiti gone missing rang familiar, and it brought the documentary about Tut I'd watched to mind. Hadn't the narrator said something about Nefertiti disappearing? Yes! He had. Nobody knew if she was murdered, abducted, or had run away, but at one point in history, she'd just vanished. She was eventually found, since her mummified body was discovered in a tomb, but no one knew for sure what had happened to her during the time she was missing.

I quickly outlined what I remembered to Grant. "Nefertiti wasn't Tut's mother. His real mother was Kiya, but she died when he was born. He was raised by Nefertiti."

Grant looked at me askance. "Since when did you become an expert on Egyptology?"

"Since I saw a documentary once on PBS, and you evidently didn't. We should go see Tut," I said.

"You don't strike me as the type to watch documentaries," he said as we trotted down the hallway toward Tut's room. We didn't know if he'd be in there, but it was as good a place as any to start looking for him.

I sniffed as if offended. "Just because I ended up at the Stanton School for Boys doesn't mean I'm stupid."

"I didn't say you were stupid. I just figured you were more the jock type. You know, football and baseball and stuff."

A jock? *Me?* I didn't even *own* a pair of cleats. "There was nothing else on TV that night. It was pretty interesting, though, I guess. It's coming in handy now, that's for sure." I cast a sideways glance at him. "What about you? I figured you for a tennis player, or that game rich guys play on horses."

He snorted. "Polo? No, the only horse I've ever been on was impaled on a pole on a carousel. I'm afraid of horses."

"No... really? Who's afraid of *horses*? They're too pretty to be scary," I said, and laughed.

He turned red and looked embarrassed, frowning. "Forget I said anything."

"Oh, come on. Don't get mad. I'm sorry." Me and my big mouth. Just when we'd been getting along again—he'd even thrown me a compliment about being a jock, although I doubted he knew he'd done it – and I blew it by laughing at him. "Really, I'm sorry. I'll bet lots of people are afraid of horses. Dogs, too. Snakes... pigeons..."

He laughed. "Nobody's afraid of *pigeons*."

"I'll bet there are some people who are." I faked a shudder. "They freak me out a little. Pigeons have that weird way of looking at you, like they know something you don't, and then they just waddle out of your way like they're not scared of you, even though you're, like, a hundred times bigger than they are."

Grant smiled. "You're a really strange person, you know that?"

"So I've been told," I answered, and returned his smile. "Me, now, I'm claustrophobic. If you ever really want to see a freak show, try locking me in a closet."

"I thought you were already in a closet," he retorted. He was grinning when he said it, and elbowed me for good measure.

My jaw practically hit the floor. *Wow. I guess he's figured out that I'm into guys. Well,* I thought, *at least he seems cool with it.* I chuckled. "Good one," I said, bumping my shoulder into his.

We were laughing as we reached Tut's bedroom, and it took an effort for us to sober up before we went inside. The guards were gone, the doors open, and the room empty except for his servants. Maids were busily straightening Tut's room, although they looked as nervous and upset as the other's we'd seen in the hallway. Grant asked one where we could find the king.

"King Tutankhamen, may he live forever, is in the Great Hall, attending to the crisis!" the servant replied as she fluffed the pillows.

"Where's that?" I asked.

She looked at me as if I'd lost my mind. I guess everyone knew where to find the Great Hall. Personally, I thought everyone who entered the palace should've been handed a map. The place was huge.

Grant took my elbow. "I bet it's where everyone was heading yesterday, before we broke off and found Tut," he said.

It made sense. I took a quick look at the carved chest next to Tut's bed, but the amulet wasn't there. He'd probably put it on as soon as he woke up. We hurried out of Tut's bedroom and down the stairs, navigating the hallway toward the place we'd first entered the palace the day before.

The entry hall was packed with people, all of them jabbering excitedly. The immense double doors that led into the Great Hall were closed. We approached the guards who were standing there, barring anyone from entering. They stared straight ahead, barely even noticing us.

"We need to see King Tutankhamen," I said, warily eyeing the curved scimitars they held.

"The king, may he live forever, is not receiving visitors." The man's expression never changed from the fierce, stony look.

"He'll receive us. We're his friends!" I protested, in spite of my fear of being beheaded right there in the entry hall.

"Go away, *now*!" His lip curled over his teeth, and he fingered the hilt of his sword. He was obviously not in the mood to deal with teenaged strangers. "We have no time for peasants like you."

Peasants? I frowned and was about to say something that might very well have ended with me losing my head, but Grant's elbow digging into my ribs shut my mouth before the words could leave it.

"Come on," he whispered. "We'll come back later."

Grant and I backed away. "There must be another way into the Great Hall," I said, once we were out of sight and hearing of the massive guards. "I'm sure Tut doesn't use the front door every time he needs to go in there."

"Let's try this way," Grant agreed, pointing to yet another hallway leading off the main corridor.

This hallway was long and narrow, lined with busts of dead kings, statues of animal-headed gods, and paintings. We followed its twisting and turning length for several minutes until we finally found another door.

It was open, and we could hear voices from inside. We paused just out of sight, listening.

"Only the gods know why these things sometimes happen. It is best to trust the gods' judgment and let them reveal their plans in their own time." The voice was deep and gruff, and sounded irritated.

"This is not the work of the gods!" Tut was agitated and angry. I could hear it in his voice. "The gods will make the Nile flood, or not, or make the crops wither, or not. They do not make a person disappear!"

"Do you dare speak for the gods, little king?"

My hands tightened into fists. Who was this jerk to speak to Tut that way? I glanced at Grant and saw the same expression of anger on his face.

"You forget your place, Aye. *You* are Grand Vizier. *I* am Pharaoh! I am divine by birth! Unless, perhaps, you wish it were otherwise?"

I was amazed at the power in Tut's voice. There was a definite hint of sarcasm in his last question. It reminded me that Tut wasn't just another kid like me and Grant. He was Pharaoh of Egypt, and his word was law. Aye must have heard it, too, because when he spoke again, it was in a much more restrained tone.

"Of course, my Lord. My apologies. I forgot myself in my distress," Aye said.

I didn't believe a word of it. Aye sounded condescending, as if he just patronized Tut. I wondered if Tut heard it. I risked a quick peek into the room. Aye was an older man, with deeply tanned, leathery skin and a body just beginning to show its age. He wore a kilt, and a wide collar made of gold. A whip was curled at his side.

I could see Tut, too. A tall conical hat sat on his head, and he wore a ridiculous (to my eyes, anyway) false beard strapped to his chin. He was sitting on his throne, on an elevated platform. Aye stood before him.

"I want the palace searched again, and the whole of the city next. Go house to house, if you must. We *will* find Nefertiti!" Tut hissed.

"As you wish it, so it will be done," Aye said. I heard sandals clicking on tile, fading away. When I was sure Aye had left, I risked a longer peek into the Great Hall.

Tut was sitting on a wide, golden bench on what looked like a small stage, surrounded by servants and piles of treasure too numerous for me to take in all at one glance. There were piles of gleaming gold rings and statuettes, bolts of different colored cloths, goblets, dishes, bowls, urns, giant ostrich eggs, curving ivory tusks, and many other fabulous objects.

He was leaning forward, his arms resting on his lap, holding a flail in one hand and a small shepherd's crook in the other. He looked just like the image I'd seen of him on his sarcophagus in that documentary I'd watched. His braids fell over one shoulder, hiding his face, but when he looked up as we entered the room, they fell away. No one had done his eye makeup, and for a brief minute, he looked like a lonely, scared kid. I noticed he was wearing the amulet.

"My friends! You have heard the terrible news?" he asked, gesturing for us to come closer.

"We heard that Nefertiti has gone missing," I said, refraining from saying what I'd been thinking... that her tomb had been found with her in it, three thousand years later.

"She is the only mother I know," Tut said sadly. "She ruled in my stead until I was old enough to take the crown. It is she who often aids me when I must make important decisions. I value her advice." He glanced toward the double doors, and lowered his voice. "Aye wishes me to believe it is the gods' will that she is gone, but I sense the hand of man in this!"

I was willing to bet Nefertiti was all that stood between Aye and the boy who sat on the throne of Egypt, and knew in that moment that, although Tut didn't say it, he loved her as much as any son loved his mother. I felt a stab of jealousy and wished my relationship with my own stepmother was as close. It wasn't Tut's fault that my stepmom didn't like me. Besides, if I was really truthful, I would admit that I hadn't given her much to like. All she'd really gotten from me was a smart-mouthed kid who was always getting in trouble. I wondered if I gave her half a chance if things could be different between us.

Shaking my head, I focused on Tut's problem, not my own. "I think you might be right," I answered, keeping my voice down. "Do you trust him, Tut? That Aye guy, I mean."

"Aye is my Grand Vizier. His advice has also helped me rule since I was but a boy. He was a trusted general of my father's."

"That's not really answering my question," I pointed out. "He didn't sound too respectful when we overheard him talking to you before."

Tut looked away for a moment, then turned back to face me. "Sometimes, I fear Aye harbors heresy in his heart," Tut admitted. "I do not wish to believe it of him, but there have been whispers among the palace servants that he covets the throne for himself. Sometimes he speaks to me as if I am still a child."

"You need to be really careful, Tut. A man like that might do anything to get what he wants," I said. I didn't want to come right out and tell Tut that Aye might end up murdering him in a couple of years, because I knew Tut would never believe me. "It seems to me he'd want to hunt for Nefertiti before blaming it on the gods."

"Tut, is there anywhere Nefertiti might go? I mean, places she liked to visit?" Grant asked.

"Not alone, and never without telling anyone she was leaving. Her servants said she went to sleep last night, but this morning, when they went into her room with food to break her fast, she was gone," Tut said. "Her guards swear they saw nothing. I have ordered that the usual places—the banks of the river where she likes to swim, the homes of friends with whom she likes to visit—be checked, but so far, none have seen her."

"What about her room?" Grant asked next.

"What of it?" Tut looked from Grant to me, but I was as clueless as Tut.

"In our country, we take a good look at the place the person was last seen for clues. Sometimes, it gives us a good idea about what happened. Was there any sign of a struggle? Was there any... blood?" Grant asked.

Tut looked surprised. "I have not seen her room for myself. Aye had Nefertiti's maids clean her room for her eventual return. He said nothing was out of order."

"How convenient," I said under my breath, but I know Grant heard me from the expression on his face. The more I heard, the more I thought Aye might be behind Nefertiti's disappearance. "Maybe you should question her maids."

Tut nodded and clapped for a servant, ordering him to bring Nefertiti's maids to the Great Hall. The servant scampered off quickly.

My stomach, never known to have terrific timing, chose that moment to grumble loudly.

"My apologies. No one has so much as offered you a fig this morning to break your fast, have they? Please, eat," Tut said, gesturing toward a table laden with food. Grant and I made a beeline for the banquet, stuffing ourselves silly with fruit and bread, and drinking milk sweetened with honey. I brought a cup of it, and a hunk of bread slathered with honey, over to Tut.

"I'll bet you haven't eaten, either," I said, handing him the goblet and slice of bread.

He took it gratefully, smiling. "You are a good friend, Ass."

Okay, I could've done without being called "Ass" again, but I was glad Tut thought of me as a friend. Then I noticed Grant frowning at me, and wondered what that was all about.

"Suck up," he muttered, low enough for only me to hear.

"*Shut* up," I hissed, equally as softly. "I was just being nice."

"You *like* him," I thought I heard Grant grumble, but I convinced myself I was mistaken. Why would Grant care if I liked Tut?

It was food for thought, though. Was Grant just

concerned about me postponing stealing Tut's amulet if I had a crush on Tut? Or was something else bugging him?

I didn't have a crush on Tut, not really. It was Grant who I kept thinking about, but I wasn't about to admit it. Still, as I helped myself to another piece of bread, chewing slowly, I watched Grant out of the corner of my eye. He seemed to be watching me back, casting furtive glances in my direction, then turning away when he saw me looking. He seemed angry.

Or could it be jealousy I saw in his darkened expression? *Nah,* I told myself, *don't be stupid. You're reading things into it that don't exist.*

I didn't have time to think about it anymore, because at that moment Nefertiti's servants arrived, and things got deadly serious.

Chapter Ten

The servants who'd attended Nefertiti, three girls, came into the Great Hall in the company of a pair of guards. None of the girls were older than fifteen or sixteen, and they looked positively terrified.

"Tell me what you saw when you first discovered all was not right with your mistress," Tut said. He drained the last of the milk I'd given him and handed the empty goblet to me. I placed it back on the table, trying to make it less obvious that I was listening.

The girls fell to the floor, pressing their faces to the marble, shaking but silent. "W-we did only as the Grand Vizier ordered us to do, my Pharaoh!" the bravest of the girls finally squealed, barely looking up at Tut. "He told us to speak to no one about what we found!"

I arched an eyebrow. *So, Aye* was *involved in some sort of cover up!* I thought. I knew I didn't trust that guy!

Tut showed remarkable restraint with the three girls, more than I would have. I would've been screaming at them. "Surely the Grand Vizier did not mean you should withhold this information from your pharaoh," he said gently. "Tell me. What did you find?"

The girls huddled on the floor. "Nefertiti was not in her bed when we arrived. The coverlets were on the floor, and her night-basket had spilled. Th-there was blood on her linens, oh, Great Pharaoh."

"The Grand Vizier told you to clean up the blood and not to tell anybody about it?" I asked. Tut raised an eyebrow toward me, but seemed to decide to allow me butting my nose into his business.

"Answer Ass. He is a Friend of Egypt," Tut ordered.

Grant coughed, but I knew he was trying to cover his laughter at hearing my "nickname" again.

Jeez. I really need to get Tut to call me something else, I thought, shooting Grant an irritated look.

"Y-yes, he did," the girl stammered. "Oh, please Great Pharaoh, do not throw us to the crocodiles!"

Wow. Guess they took crime and punishment pretty seriously in ancient Egypt, I thought. Particularly since Tut didn't laugh at her worries.

"I shall show mercy on you, since you were following the orders of the Grand Vizier," Tut said, "but never keep information such as this from me again."

He waved a hand, and the guards escorted the weeping girls out of the Grand Hall.

"Would you really have them fed to the crocs?" Grant asked, beating me to the punch.

Tut shrugged one bare shoulder, but didn't bat an eye. "Treason is punishable by death. Those guilty of it are not worthy of passing into the afterlife." He acted as if what he was suggesting happened every day of the week and was of no more significance than when the judge sentenced me to a year at the Stanton School for Boys.

I reminded myself never to cross Tut, or if I did, to be well on my way back to the present before he found out. "What do you mean, Tut?" I was almost afraid to ask.

Tut looked at me as if I was stupid. "Surely it is the same in your country? Treason against the pharaoh is the most terrible crime that can be committed. I am divine. After my death, when I pass through the shadows of the Underworld and Osiris weighs my heart and finds me worthy, I will take my place among the gods. Therefore, anyone guilty of treason is guilty of heresy. Everyone knows this. No tomb shall be erected for them, and their body shall not be mummified but left to turn to dust, blown away by the wind... or eaten by crocodiles."

Did Tut really believe he was almost a god? I looked into his dark, unflinching eyes, and saw that it was true.

Wow. Talk about having a god-complex. And here I thought Meek had been full of himself.

Still, Tut didn't act high and mighty. He didn't have to—he truly believed he was divine, and what's more, everyone else believed it, too.

"Tut, I don't think Nefertiti ran away. I think someone either took her, or..." I let my voice trail off, unwilling to say that I thought she might've been murdered.

Tut looked stricken. "Why would anyone want to hurt Nefertiti? She is quite beloved by the people."

"Maybe not by *all* of the people," I said, glancing at the double golden doors through which Aye had gone. "Maybe some people aren't happy that she sides with you all the time, or that she still advises you on matters of state."

"No, it was Nefertiti's idea to return to the old ways. My father, Akhenaten, was misguided. He destroyed the temples of the gods and forced Egypt to honor only one—Aten, god of the sun. Under Nefertiti's advice, I rebuilt the old temples and gave honor to all the gods once more. The people were grateful. No one would want to hurt her."

"Are you sure? Even somebody who might... how did

you say it? Harbor heresy in his heart?" I asked.

Tut was quick to catch on. He clapped his hands and ordered his servants and guards out of the room, leaving us alone. Still, he lowered his voice. "Surely, you do not suggest that *Aye* is behind her disappearance?"

"I think Ass may be right, Tut. It seems awfully suspicious that he knew what the maids found, and not only didn't tell you about it—in fact, made you believe she simply ran away, and that it was the will of the gods—but ordered the maids not to talk to you about it, either," Grant said. I was grateful for his support, in spite of him using Tut's nickname for me, and gave him a quick smile.

Tut cocked his head, looking at us out of the corner of his eye. "There are those who would say you are also suspicious. You came here only yester-morn. Perhaps your king sent you here to destroy me from within my own house!"

My jaw dropped. All we wanted was his amulet, not his throne! "How can you say that? I thought we were friends!"

"Likewise, I thought until today that Aye was naught but a faithful servant. Yet, as you point out, circumstances imply that he is not," Tut retorted.

"If we were going to try to hurt you, we could've done it yesterday, when we first met you in the garden. There weren't any guards there, and we were alone for a short while last night, too, in your bedroom, if you remember," Grant pointed out.

Tut smirked. "I admit you are young to be assassins," he said. "But this is what Aye will claim if I confront him with your accusations. He will have you killed, and I may not be able to protect you. He is Grand Vizier and has great power, make no mistake. He commands my legions, and makes many decisions for the good of Egypt." Tut looked away, frowning. He continued, although he seemed to be talking more to himself than to us. "He treats me as a child, telling me what he thinks I wish to hear, but doing as he pleases. I have begun to think it is time for me to fully take my place as pharaoh, including choosing a new Grand Vizier. Even my wife agrees with me on this. Nefertiti did, too."

I blinked, stunned. "Y-you have a wife? You're *married*?"

Tut looked baffled. "Of course, I married as soon as I was able to fulfill my husbandly duties. It was a prerequisite of my taking my father's crown as pharaoh." He waved a hand, dismissing my amazement. "Her name is Ankhesanamum. It was a logical match. She is my half-sister and Nefertiti's daughter. The throne of Egypt will not pass from our bloodline to another."

Ew! Yuck! I couldn't *imagine* marrying either of my half-sisters. Even if it were legal and I were straight, it was too gross for words.

For some reason, Grant looked pleased. He had a small, smug smile on his face. I frowned at him and turned my attention back to Tut. "Do you have kids, then?"

"I have many goats," Tut replied, cocking his head. "What have they to do with my wife?"

"Not goat-kids. I meant children. Do you have any children?" I clarified. I'd need to remember that modern expressions didn't mean the same thing in ancient Egypt.

A frown creased Tut's forehead. "No, she has not provided me with an heir as yet. Two girls were born, but they walk the next world now. It is another worry... I must have a son to follow me to the throne."

That could be the reason he was murdered so young—

before he could have children to inherit the throne, I thought. "I think it would wise to think about your safety, Tut."

"What do you mean?" he asked.

I still didn't want to tell him I suspected Aye of murdering him, but I was worried that the murder of Nefertiti (after hearing about the blood in her room, I was sure she was dead) was the first domino to fall in Aye's plan to become pharaoh. Tut might very well be next on Aye's hit list. "We have reason to believe that Nefertiti was at least injured, because of the blood the maids found on her bed sheets. That means that somebody in this palace was able to get past her guards and hurt her. There's no reason to believe they couldn't do the same to you," I said. I watched his expression carefully. He was at first incredulous, then slowly, understanding dawned in his eyes. He believed me, and that was important. Maybe if I could get him away from the palace, I could save his life without ever telling him what I knew about his murder.

"He's right, Tut," Grant said. "You shouldn't stay in the palace. You don't know who you can trust here in Memphis."

"Leave the city? I suppose I could, but I would need an excuse, an explanation for my absence while everyone is searching for Nefertiti..." Tut looked thoughtful for a moment. "Of course! We shall go to the pyramids at Giza as we planned. I shall say that I travel there to ask the help of the Khufu and the gods. It will not be a lie; the gods will give me a sign that will help me find Nefertiti." He said it with the utmost confidence, as if completely certain that the gods would answer his prayers.

It seemed I was going to get to see the pyramids up close and personal after all. I only hoped the trip would keep Tut safe and give Grant and me the opportunity to steal the amulet while we were at it. "When do we leave?" I asked. "The sooner the better, you know."

"Yes. We will leave this very day," Tut said. He clapped his hands for his servants and guards. "Ready the royal barge! We travel the Nile to Giza!"

Barge? Wait a minute... wasn't a barge like a boat? Tut hadn't said anything yesterday about using a boat when we talked about going to Giza. I hated boats! I got seasick just watching *movies* that took place on a ship. I remembered the funky-looking canoes we'd seen out on the river when Grant and I first arrived in Egypt. None of them looked even vaguely like anything I'd want to be sitting in on the water, especially when I knew the Nile was full of hungry crocodiles and nasty-tempered hippos!

Grant must've read my fear on my face, because he was smirking again. I swore I was *so* going to get even with him, if it was the last thing I did. "I don't suppose we'll have to ride horses to get there, will we?" I saw Grant's eyes widen and held back a laugh.

Tut looked shocked. "*Ride?* On the backs of horses? How is that possible?" He shook his head. "We will use chariots," Tut said. "Time is of the essence, and I do not wish to walk from the palace at Giza to the pyramids."

Okay. Chariots were almost as good as having to ride horses, I thought, watching Grant's face pale. It would be worth a boat ride to see Grant on the back of a chariot, trying to control a horse—if I didn't drown first, or get eaten by crocs or hippos before we got there, of course.

Suddenly, I didn't feel so smug after all.

Chapter Eleven

When I saw Tut again, he'd taken off the cone-shaped hat and fake beard. I was glad; the costume made him look ridiculous to me, although I'm sure the Egyptians didn't think so. Someone had painted his eyes, rimming them in dark green and gray, and his cheeks and lips were touched with red. He was dressed in a new, bright white, pleated kilt, and wore his amulet, along with a heavy, wide necklace of gold. A belt of the same precious metal, studded with gems, was wrapped around his narrow hips. Golden armbands encircled his biceps and ankles. A headdress made of small, flat, linked pieces of gold covered his head, and fell to brush his shoulders. A cobra's head (I was willing to bet it was molded from solid gold, too, like everything else—Tut really was the bling king) was mounted on the hat over the center of Tut's forehead. It had ruby eyes that glittered in the sunlight.

Four servants stood by a long, low lounge chair piled with pillows and shaded by a white awning. Once Tut was comfortably seated on it, they picked the entire thing up and carried him out of the palace, through the city, to the riverbank. Grant and I followed along behind the lounge.

To my surprise, the servants didn't put him down when

they reached the water's edge. Instead, they carried both him and the chair into the water all the way to the barge, which floated just offshore on the river. They were very careful to keep Tut's chair above water. I could see their muscles straining at the combined weight of the chair and Tut. I was almost surprised that he didn't sink the damn ship when he finally got off the chair and stepped onto the barge with all of the gold he was wearing. The servants heaved the lounge aboard and placed it near the center of the barge.

Grant and I were not offered a ride to the barge. We waded through the river just like everyone else. I moved as quickly as I could through the water, keeping a sharp eye out for the crocodiles and hippos I was sure were lurking just beneath the surface. We were both soaked from the waist down by the time we heaved ourselves aboard.

Tut's barge was a lot bigger than I'd thought at first. It was a low, wide boat that narrowed to curving points at both ends. There were several rows of flat bench seats on either side, and many long oars that poked down into the water. Each seat was taken by two strong-looking men, their hands already wrapped around the oars as if waiting for Tut's order to begin rowing.

Archers stood at the prow and stern, ready to defend the king should anybody be foolish enough to attack the barge. They were each equipped with a carved bow and a quiver of arrows strapped to their backs.

We wrung out our kilts as best we could and walked to the middle of the barge, where Tut lay, comfortable—and dry—on his lounge. Two servants stood at his elbow, ready to get him a drink, or something to eat, or swat bugs and wave away the heat with big ostrich feather fans, at his command.

To my amazement, another servant smeared honey on himself, covering his chest, shoulders, and arms with a thick layer of the gooey, yellow sweet. When a fly landed on him and got stuck, I realized what the purpose of the honey was... he was ancient Egyptian human fly paper!

Some people really have the life, I thought, then winced as I remembered Tut's life might be over in just a couple of years, if not sooner.

Tut motioned for us to take seats next to his lounge. I sat down as close to the center as I could (I figured if the boat sank, I could grab hold of Tut's lounge and float) and got comfortable, watching the men at the heavy oars. The muscles in their backs and arms bulged with effort as they began pulling and pushing, and the barge began to slowly slice smoothly through the water.

A very large, barrel-chested man who wore a whip curled at his side stood between the two rows of rowers and began to sing. Actually, it wasn't really *singing*; it was more like a chant, and the oars moved in time to the cadence. I guessed its purpose was to keep the rowers all moving at the same time. Forward, back. Forward, back. The big man would chant a verse, and the rowers would answer with the chorus. It was a song about the gods of Egypt, and I caught the names Ra, Isis, Osiris, and Anubis.

People on the shore stopped what they were doing as we passed, waving and shouting. I could see them lift small children to their shoulders, and some waded out into the water to get a better look. It was kind of like being in a parade, and I grinned and waved back at them, even though I knew it wasn't me they were looking at, but Tut.

He ignored them all with the air of somebody who'd been there, done that. I guess Tut was like celebrities in my own time, the ones who always had fans staring at them and paparazzi hovering around, snapping photos. Tut looked a little bored with the whole thing.

It was cooler on the river with the breeze of the moving barge blowing in our hair, and as time passed, I began to forget my fear of boats and enjoy the ride. I stared out at the water and caught glimpses of sharp-toothed, scaly crocs sunning on the banks, and the huge, broad backs of hippos in the water. One head broke the surface of the water, and it roared a warning at us, showing us its cavernous mouth and four giant, spiked, ivory teeth. The archers turned as one toward the hippo. I guess if it had come any closer to the barge, they would have shot it.

I'd always thought hippopotamuses were cute with their big, fat bodies and tiny little ears, like the dancing one in the tutu in the Disney cartoons, but I'd learned from Tut that they killed more people every year than the scarier-looking crocodiles. Seeing them up close and personal brought that home to me. They were not cuddly at all. They looked as nasty as their tempers when you saw them at close range, and I was very glad when we left the herd of hippos behind.

After a long while, the ride began to get boring. Imagine riding in a slow-moving car for hours without a handheld video game or MP3 player. The scenery all starts to look the same, mile after mile. I decided it was time for a little conversation, although I knew there were too many listening ears around us, and the subject of Nefertiti and Aye would be off limits until the three of us were alone. I wondered what we should talk about, and looked up at Tut. That's when I noticed his color-rimmed eyes again.

"Why do Egyptians use makeup?" I asked. "In our country, women use makeup, and some men, but here it seems everybody does, from little kids right on up to the old people." I noticed Grant looking at Tut, too. He must have been wondering the same thing.

"How very backward your people must be!" Tut exclaimed. "Everyone knows there are many reasons. First, we invoke the protection of Ra by imitating his Great Eye," he said, gesturing toward his own eye makeup, "but we must also protect ourselves from the strength of his sun. Painting our eyes does both. Plus, it helps protect us from the evil eye, curses sent by our enemies. And, it makes us look pretty, doesn't it?" He laughed and swatted at a fly that had out-maneuvered the ostrich feather fans. "It also helps keep away biting insects! *Udju* and *mesdemet* are truly a gift of the gods," he added, using the Egyptian names Merlin's instant translation spell told me meant green malachite and lead ore.

"Ancient sunblock and insect repellant!" I heard Grant whisper. I nodded. It was a very smart thing to do, considering they lived in a desert. "I *still* think they look like drag queens," Grant said under his breath, and I choked back a laugh.

Tut pointed off into the distance. "There are the three Great Pyramids, the tombs of the pharaohs before me. We have an old saying: *Everything fears time, but time fears the pyramids.* They have stood on the sand for a thousand years, and will stand for ten thousand more. My own tomb will be equally grand. When the time comes for me to enter the Underworld and have Osiris weigh my heart against the Feather of Truth, I will arrive as I live now, with all of my wealth, and because of this the people of Egypt will live in prosperity." He seemed at ease to be talking about his death, but it made me uncomfortable, considering I knew that, unless I could do something to prevent it, death would be coming for him far sooner than Tut realized.

I stared at the pyramids which were, essentially, the three largest tombstones in the world. "So, what do you do for fun here?" I asked next. I was reminded again that ancient Egypt had no television, no MP3s, no movies... I couldn't imagine what Tut did when he got bored.

"We play games like Senet, and Hounds and Jackals, celebrate festivals, and of course, we have dancers and musicians at the palace," Tut replied. "Surely they have these things in your country?"

"Yeah, we have that stuff, too," I replied, thinking about my Wii at home, and the hours I'd spent playing Rock Band with my friends. I didn't elaborate since I knew he wouldn't understand the concept of video games, peripherals, and rock music legends. I knew Tut's version of a board game wouldn't be like Scrabble or Monopoly, either. I figured it was more like Stratego or backgammon, neither of which I was particularly good at.

Time passed slowly, and even though the breeze was cooler on the moving barge, the heat of the day began to make me feel drowsy. My head drooped as my eyelids grew heavy, and I must have drifted off, because the next thing I knew, Grant was poking me in the shoulder.

"Wake up, Aston!" Poke, poke, poke.

I tried to slap his hand away. "Sleeping. Leave me alone."

"Wake up," he said. "You were talking in your sleep! Anyway, we're almost there."

My eyelids fluttered open, and I sat up straight.

"What? Where's here?" I was confused, and couldn't remember where I was for a minute. I realized the barge had stopped, and without the cooler river breeze, the heat was incredible.

Grant snorted. "We're at the North Pole. Don't you feel how cold it is? We're almost in Giza, remember? King Tut? Merlin and needing to get his you-know-what?"

I came fully awake and scowled at him. "Tell me, were you born this sarcastic, or is it an implant?"

He sniffed and raised an eyebrow. "Oh, I'm *always* sarcastic, and you're always an idiot. So tell me, who exactly *was* it that you were kissing in your dream?"

I felt my cheeks heat with a furious flush that had nothing to do with the sweltering heat, because I could tell from his wicked little smile that I must've said a name aloud while I'd been sleeping.

He already knew who I'd been kissing in my dream.

Him.

I wanted to jump overboard and throw myself at the first herd of hippos I could find. I was never going to live this down, never!

Chapter Twelve

I was saved from trying to feed myself to the hippos by our arrival at Giza.

The riverbank here was nothing like the bustling beach at Memphis. There were very few people washing or fishing; I suppose not many folks wanted to live in the shadow of three tombstones, no matter how great the pharaohs whose bodies lay buried there had been. It would be like living next to a graveyard... a little too creepy for my tastes, anyway. Plus, Memphis was where the pharaoh lived, and that's where all the activity was centered. I supposed it would be like comparing New York City or Washington D.C. with any small town in the U.S. If you wanted peace and quiet, you moved to the suburbs. If you wanted glamour and excitement, you got an apartment in the city.

The pyramids were much closer, of course, and just as I'd suspected, they were enormous. Rising above the desert dunes and small town set back from the river, they were gleaming brilliant white in the sun. The very tip of the largest one, the Great Pyramid of Khufu, glittered gold as the light caught it. I had to admit—even if it was just to me—that it was pretty cool to see them for real and not just as a picture in a book.

We could see the Sphinx from the river, too. With the

head of a man and the body of a lion, it reminded me of a gigantic chess piece sitting there. I could almost imagine a colossal hand reaching down from the sky and moving it across a board only the gods could see.

Chess! Jeez. Was I turning into a geek, or what? It was as if being sent back into time was sucking the coolness right out of me. If I wasn't careful, I'd be quoting Shakespeare and crap before I knew it.

I risked a glance at Grant, even though I really didn't want to talk to him at the moment. I was still too embarrassed over him overhearing me mumble in my sleep that I was kissing him to chance drawing him into a conversation.

It'd been a really good dream, too; at least, what I could remember of it. We were at the lake near my hometown, and were floating on a wide raft, just him and me. It was hot, and we were in our swimsuits. He looked really good in his, I remember. We were just lying there, and I looked over at him, and then suddenly, we were kissing.

You know how it is in dreams... things never happen in them like they do in real life. I knew we'd probably never be at the lake together, or lying on a raft, and certainly not sucking face. Still, it was a really good kiss, and a really good dream, and I was a little pissed at Grant for ruining it for me by busting my chops about it.

He was too busy staring at the pyramids to notice me, though. His green eyes were as wide as saucers, and his mouth was hanging open. I was almost praying for a fly to zip in there, just so I'd have something to tease *him* about.

Tut's litter bearers, as the men who carried his lounge were called, hoisted him up onto their shoulders again and carried him off the barge, sloshing through the water to the shore. Grant hopped over the side into the water and followed him without hesitation.

I wasn't quite so quick to jump in with both feet. Instead, I took a minute and leaned over the edge of the boat, scanning the water for crocs. I hadn't come this far only to end up as lunch for a crocodile.

The coast looked clear, or at least, croc-free. I lowered myself into the warm water and waded to the beach. My kilt kept floating up, and I spent most of the time it took me to get to land batting at it, trying to keep it down. After all, the only thing Merlin had given us in the way of underwear was a tiny loincloth that looked a lot like a g-string and didn't cover very much. I didn't want the fish to get an eyeful of any dangly bits that might make them think I was serving dinner.

We followed Tut's litter over the beach toward the sand dunes. There was a path paved with smooth rocks, so the walking wasn't difficult, but it was so hot out that, by the time we finally reached anything that resembled civilization, my kilt was completely dry, and I was sweating.

Tut's home here at Giza was nothing like his palace in Memphis. It was much smaller, more like a country house, I suppose. There was plenty of treasure here, too—I guess a king needed to keep up appearances and all no matter where he was living—but not nearly as much as in the palace. There were statues and vases scattered all around, and carved and painted furniture, but it seemed almost bare bones after experiencing the wealth at Tut's palace in Memphis.

Grant and I were each given our own rooms, for which I was grateful. While I liked Grant (maybe a little more than I should, actually, considering my dreams), a guy needed his privacy now and then. My room was small, with a long, low couch that served as a bed. There was a garden just outside my window, filled with colorful flowers and birds.

I realized one of the problems with having windows but no glass was that anything *outside* could very easily find its way *inside*. Since I'd arrived in ancient Egypt, I'd scored dozens of mosquito and fly bites. They itched, and it wasn't as if I could run to the infirmary or drug store to buy calamine lotion or bug repellant. Layer that itching on top of my sunburn, and before I knew it, I'd become a scratching, peeling mess.

Add being tired from the boat ride and walk from the beach, and I was asleep before my body hit the bed. I don't know how long I slept, but when a servant came in to wake me, the sun was nearly set, and it was much cooler.

Tut and Grant were waiting for me in the gardens. A table had been set with fruit, meat, and some kind of fermented beverage that Tut called "beer," although it didn't look like any beer I'd ever seen before. The meat was unidentifiable. It could've been roasted crocodile butt for all I knew, but it tasted okay, and I was hungry.

At one point, a servant came over and placed a small, perfumed cone of some sort of brownish material that reminded me of incense on top of our heads. It seemed like a really weird thing for somebody to do, but Tut didn't blink an eye at it, so I chalked it up to being another ancient custom and let it be. After a while, the cones began to melt, filling the air with the smell of flowers. It actually felt kind of good... it cooled off my scalp, at least, but I still thought it was the most bizarre party hat I'd ever worn, and I was very glad nobody at home could see me sitting there with an incense cone balanced on top of my head.

There was little conversation over dinner, but when we were through and the servants had cleared our plates, Tut sent them away. He leaned forward, resting his elbows on the table. The look on his face was serious, and I knew what was coming.

"Aye will not be happy that I chose to leave the palace without informing him. He will come here after me, I am sure, and I wish to know your suspicions before he arrives," Tut said.

"I don't like him," Grant said. "There's something about him that I don't trust."

"Me, either," I agreed. "I think he wants to be pharaoh, Tut."

Tut laughed, waving a hand dismissively in the air. "That is ridiculous! Aye is my most trusted advisor. He was my guiding hand when I was young, and helped me earn my throne. What you accuse him of is heresy!"

"You told us before that you suspected Aye might not be on the up and up... er... harboring heresy in his heart," Grant said. "I think you were right about that."

"Exactly. You should trust your instincts, Tut. Look, you listened to his advice when you were young, right?" I persisted.

"Of course. I was a child, and he was older and wiser," Tut said.

I exchanged a glance with Grant. We were going to be entering dangerous territory. Tut obviously respected and maybe loved Aye as a father figure, and what I was about to tell him might make Tut angry and defensive. "In other words, he suggested the policies and whatever, and you made them into law?"

Tut nodded. He cocked his head, obviously not quite able to understand where my logic was going.

"Don't you see? Aye *ruled*, Tut. You had the name and the crown and stuff, but he made the laws!" Grant said.

"Right," I added. "Now that you're older, you're starting to make your own decisions. I don't think he likes that very much. Before, Nefertiti let him put his ideas into your head, but now she wants you to become the pharaoh she knows you could be. I don't think Aye liked that either."

Tut shook his head. "No, I do not wish to believe this. Aye wishes only the best for me." I could see that he was getting a little angry, probably because we were talking crap about the man who had stepped in as his father after Tut's real dad died. It was one thing if *he* said it and another if *we* did. Nobody likes to hear their family dissed.

"I think Aye wishes only the best for himself," I said. I put up a hand before he could disagree. "You asked for our opinion and we're giving it, that's all. Besides, you said yourself that you've heard rumors at the palace about Aye wanting the throne."

"Actually, while we're on the subject, I know she's your stepmom… er, second mother, but Nefertiti liked power, too," Grant said. "She ruled for a while, didn't she? After your dad died, but before you were crowned pharaoh?"

Tut's face darkened. He looked offended. "She did. She changed her name to 'Smenkhkare' and held the crook and flail for a short while. What are you suggesting?"

"Only that she wouldn't want Aye to sit on the throne. At least with *you* there, she would know her ideas would be heard. Chances are good that Aye wouldn't want to listen to her."

"But Nefertiti is gone! That is why we came here, because the maids confessed to finding blood in her room," Tut argued.

"That's just it! Nefertiti has been pushing for you to take the throne fully, right? Aye wouldn't have liked that, Tut. He likes having your ear, and likes that you take his suggestions. He certainly must not have liked it when Nefertiti was on the throne. She wouldn't have listened to him like you do. That's why he pushed to have you take the crown even though you were still a kid! With her out of the way, he can keep things as they are. And if something happened to you...?" My voice trailed off, leaving the darkest of my thoughts hanging in the air, unspoken.

Tut paled, his eyes widening as he finally caught on, and he gaped at us. "You think Aye *murdered* Nefertiti? And that he might wish to do the same to *me*? This is a very serious allegation, my friend. It borders on treason," he said, lowering his voice to a whisper. I guessed that he was afraid someone might overhear our conversation and get word back to Aye. Even here, in the boondocks of ancient Egypt, the walls had ears.

"Think about it, Tut. With Nefertiti gone, who would be next in line for the throne of Egypt if something happened to you?"

His face paled further as he stared at us in shock. "Aye would never—I cannot believe he would..."

Grant and I wisely remained silent, letting Tut work out the possibilities in his head. It must've been really rough for him. After all, it would be bad enough to find out that the people you trusted most may have been playing you for a fool, but it must suck the big fat one to hear that one of them was plotting to murder you.

Although I knew in my heart that I'd been sort of a jerk ever since my mom died, and especially since my dad remarried, and I knew my dad was embarrassed by the crap I'd done and my trouble with the law, I also knew he loved me and would stick by me no matter what. And even though my stepmom barely acknowledged me half of the time, and was a pain in my sphincter the other half, I believed she loved my dad, and he, for whatever reason, loved her, and neither of them would try to hurt me intentionally.

Tut was silent for a long time. I picked at some fruit, exchanging worried glances with Grant. Would Tut believe us? Even though I knew what we'd said made sense to him—enough for him to give our opinions serious thought—we were still strangers, after all. I couldn't say with any certainty that *I* would've believed us, had I been in his sandals.

"I must have proof," Tut finally said. "If what you say is true, then I must catch Aye in a lie, or obtain some other form of proof that he wishes me ill. It is the only way I can be certain that he does not have my welfare and the best interests of Egypt at heart."

It isn't exactly the response I hoped for, but at least he hasn't called for the guards and cried, "Off with their heads!" I thought. "How can we get that sort of proof, Tut? He's too smart to just out-and-out admit that he's thinking about killing you."

"On the morrow, we will go to the Great Pyramid as we had planned, and leave an offering to my ancestor, the great king, Khufu. I will pray to the gods to give me the proof I need," Tut said. He seemed completely convinced that his plan would work, that the gods themselves would present him with evidence of Aye's guilt or innocence.

I wondered how he thought this proof would come to him. Would he see visions in the clouds, or in the sand? Would it come in a dream? It didn't seem likely that any sign he received would *actually* come from the gods. How many men's lives had been lost or destroyed because a king thought he had a direct phone line to the Great Hereafter? He might as well call the Psychic Hotline for answers.

Tut believed it, though, and there was nothing I could say or do to change his mind, even if I could get him to listen.

Chapter Thirteen

I'd just gotten comfortable—or as close to it as I could manage, given that my mattress was made of pillows stuffed with some sort of grass that rustled every time I moved—when Grant poked his head into my room.

"Hey, are you asleep?"

"If I was, would it matter?" I asked. I was feeling a little edgy. Not only was my bed noisy, but my bug bites were itching up a storm. I felt sure I'd scratched hard enough to draw blood. "What do you want, Grant?"

He came into my room and sat down on the edge of my bed. Something was bugging him; I could that right off. "What are we going to do about the amulet?"

"What do mean, '*do*' about the amulet? We're going to get it," I said.

"Really? Because you've been acting like you forgot all about it." He was glaring at me as if I'd done something wrong. "You seem to be concentrating more on proving to Tut that Aye is out to get him than figuring out a way to get the amulet."

"Do you think I'm stupid? I know the amulet is what we came here for."

"Do you know what I *really* think? I think you like Tut too much. I think maybe you don't want to go back at all!" he hissed.

"I do too want to go back! Do you think I *want* to be stuck here in the past with no running water, or television, or video games? Do you think I *like* stepping in goat crap every time I turn around? Look at me! I'm covered in bug bites!" I narrowed my eyes at him. "Why do you care if I like Tut, anyway?"

He turned his face away, so I couldn't read his expression. "I couldn't care less how you feel about Tut. I just want to get the amulet and go home."

"Is it the gay thing? Is that what's got your boxers in a knot?"

He looked back at me and seemed genuinely surprised. "No! I mean, I don't care about... That's not it."

"I think it is. I think that if Tut was a girl, you'd be cool with it. Admit it! You can't stand that I like Tut, and we're both guys!"

"That isn't it! You're an idiot, do you know that? A walking, talking butthole. I can't believe I even let Merlin talk me into *doing* this with you!" He got up and began heading for the door. "I'm ending this right now!"

Alarms went off in my head. If Grant did something stupid, like jump Tut and try to take the amulet from around his neck, Tut might have us killed as traitors before Merlin could whisk us home! I jumped off the bed and ran after Grant, grabbing his arm and spun him around. "Where are you going? What are you going to do?"

He yanked his arm away from me. His back was against my bedroom door, and our faces were only inches apart. He pulled his head back, and it hit the door with a good, solid *thunk*. "Back off, Aston!"

"Not until you tell me what you're going to do!" I pressed closer, trying to intimidate him. Unfortunately, I could feel the heat of his skin against my bare chest, which made other parts of me sit up and take notice. He smelled good, too, and his skin looked shiny; he must have used some of the oils the Egyptians used on their skin. He also needed a shave, the same as me, something that wasn't going to happen for either of us since the Egyptians had yet to invent a triple blade with aloe, and neither of us was about to let anyone near our throats with a knife. Sexy, dark stubble dusted his cheeks.

His eyes snapped with anger, and he gave me a push. "I said, back off!"

I pushed him back. Somewhere deep in the back of my little pea brain a light went off (wasn't this how we'd ended up in this mess to begin with?), but I ignored it. "What is wrong with you? You were fine at dinner, now all of a sudden you're acting like a jerk!"

"Yeah, well, if you stopped trying to make out with Tut all the time and thought more about how to get his amulet, we'd be home by now!" He pushed me again, and I lost my balance, falling to the floor. I managed to grab his arm on the way and pulled him down with me. We landed in a tangle of arms and legs. My back hit the hard floor, and I grunted in pain. "Get off me!" I yelled.

I heaved with all my strength and managed to get up into a half-sitting position, but Grant shoved me back down again before I could wriggle out from under him.

Grant pinned me to the floor, glaring down at me. I cursed and tried to push him off, and when that failed, tried furiously to wiggle out from underneath. I couldn't free myself, no matter how hard I tried. He had his full weight pressing down on me, and since he was a bit taller and weighed a little more than I did, I was having a hard time budging him.

His green eyes had gone dark with anger, and his lips were curled over his teeth. I'd never seen him look so furious, not even when we were fighting in Merlin's office. He looked as if he would like nothing better than to rip me to pieces with his bare hands. I think he was in the middle of an adrenaline rush, and that's what gave him the strength to keep me pinned—or at least, that was what I told myself. I didn't want to admit that he was just stronger than me.

I was absolutely certain that he was going to haul off and slug me, and my entire body tightened as if to ward off the blow that I was positive was coming. I took a deep breath and squeezed my eyes shut, waiting for him to pull his arm back and plow his fist into my face.

He didn't.

A full minute ticked by. I cracked one eye open, expecting to see his fist zooming in, but to my surprise, he didn't hit me.

Instead, he lowered his head and kissed me. There was a lot of anger in his kiss—it was almost as if he slugged me with his mouth. He kissed me so hard that I could feel his teeth pressing against my lips.

It was over just as quickly as it had happened. His head jerked up, his eyes wide, and he pushed away from me as if he couldn't wait to put distance between us. He scooted away on his butt until his back hit the door. I could see he was breathing hard, and he looked scared. "Oh, God... I'm sorry! I'm sorry, Aston. I'm sorry..."

"For what?" I asked, sitting up, feeling as stunned as he looked. I rubbed my lips absently with my fingers. They tingled, in a good way.

"For... you know... doing *that*," he said lamely. "I didn't mean to, I swear!"

"Didn't mean to do *what*? Be an idiot about Tut and body slam me to the floor, or for trying to bash my face in with your mouth?" My lips were still tickly from his kiss, brutal though it was. I realized I wanted him to kiss me again, although I wasn't about to tell him that.

"Yeah, that last one. I. Um. We..."

"Full sentences would really help in this situation, Grant," I said, still touching my mouth. He'd kissed me so hard I was afraid my lips would swell up. "Forget it. It's not a big deal."

"Not a big deal?" he gasped. "I *kissed* you!"

"That wasn't a kiss. That was a roundhouse punch by way of your lips."

"I'm sorry!"

"Stop apologizing! Jeez, Grant, it was only a kiss. It's no biggie. I just wish you'd lay off about me and Tut. Yeah, I think he's kind of hot, but there's nothing going on between us. I want to get the amulet as much as you do, and go home."

Grant looked totally miserable. "I know, I know. There's got to be something wrong with me. I never did that before! I don't know why I'm feeling all..."

"Jealous?" I finished, smirking a little.

"No!"

"Your lips say otherwise."

"I... I..."

He's really cute when he gets all flustered, I thought. His cheeks flushed red, and his eyes got big and round, but he really looked scared and confused. I decided to cut him some slack. I picked myself up from the floor, wincing at the way my back ached, and extended a hand to him. "Listen, Grant, it's okay. We'll pretend it never happened, all right?"

He stared at my outstretched hand as if it was a cobra ready to strike, but then slowly took it, and let me pull him to his feet. He wouldn't look me in the eye, though. "We *have* to go home, Aston. Everything is too weird here. It's making me crazy."

"You're not crazy." I studied him for a minute, wondering if he really liked me, or if it was as he said, just a product of the general lunacy of our situation. I decided it wasn't fair to push him about it. If he was in the closet, it wasn't up to me to pull him out, and if not, if it *was* a mistake, well, then it wasn't cool for me to bust his chops about it, either.

I found that I was really, *really* pulling for the first explanation, though.

"Look, accidents happen, and we're both tired. Let's get some sleep. Tomorrow, we're going to the Great Pyramid with Tut. We'll figure out a way to snatch the amulet while we're there, I promise." I said.

He looked miserable but nodded, turning and opening the door. As he slipped out of my room, he mumbled something under his breath that I didn't quite catch.

I thought it sounded like he'd said, "It wasn't an accident, and I'm not really sorry," but I couldn't decide if he'd really said it, or if it was just wishful thinking on my part.

I was smiling as I lay back down on the bed. It was a long time before I finally fell asleep because I kept replaying the kiss in my head, over and over again. Had he *meant* to kiss me, despite what he'd said afterward? Was he jealous because I thought Tut was hot? Was that *really* the cause of our argument, and not because Grant thought I was putting off trying to take the amulet?

Somehow, I got the feeling that it was.

Whether or not Grant wanted to admit it to himself, he *liked* me, and not just in a "let's be friends" sort of way.

I wondered what he'd do if *I* kissed *him*?

I grinned at the ceiling as I pondered what Grant was thinking about at that very moment. My money was on him reliving our kiss, too. I couldn't help but hope he was thinking about doing it again.

When I finally drifted off to sleep, my dreams were full of scenarios to that effect, and in every one of them, I kissed Grant, and he kissed me right back.

Chapter Fourteen

When we met for breakfast the next morning, Grant looked terrible. There were dark smudges under his eyes, and he looked so tired that I wondered if he'd gotten any sleep at all, although he actually gave me a small smile as he reached for a piece of bread on the table. I took that as a good sign that he was coming to terms with what had happened between us. I hoped he was accepting his attraction to me, because the more I thought about it, the more I realized that I was really starting to like him.

Tut must've slept like a rock, because he was a bundle of energy. He ate quickly and seemed impatient for us to do the same. "Come, come!" he said the minute Grant and I had choked down the last of our fruit and drained a glass of milk each.

I was certain the milk hadn't come from cows, by the way, since I had seen neither hide nor horns of any, or heard a single moo since we'd arrived in Egypt. It could have been goat milk or hippo milk for all I knew. It was always served warm, was frothy, and tasted a little sweet. I would have preferred water or fruit juice—or better yet, a Coke. Since my chances of finding a soda machine in ancient Egypt were... let me think... *zero*, and there wasn't any water or juice at the table that morning, I drank the milk.

"I am anxious to ask the gods for the proof I need," Tut said as I finished my milk and wiped a foamy mustache from my upper lip with the back of my hand. "It will take a short while to reach the Great Pyramid. We must leave now. I do not wish to be traveling during the hottest part of the day."

Grant looked at me and rolled his eyes. Neither of us was looking forward to a long walk over hot sand, under the broiling Egyptian sun. I remembered what Tut had said about using chariots, and wondered if he'd arranged to have some for our use, or if only Tut would ride to the pyramids.

Lucky for us—or unlucky, in Grant's case—Tut had no intention of letting *any* of us walk.

Tut's servants helped him dress in a loose-fitting white robe and the standard cloth headdress. When we followed him outside, the robe billowed when the breeze caught its folds, reminding me of sheets hung out on a laundry line.

I heard Grant gasp before I saw them.

Six horses were lined up outside Tut's house. Each team of two was attached by a system of leather straps to an honest-to-goodness chariot.

The chariots looked just like they did in the movies. Well, sort of. Two of them were kind of plain. They were carved from wood and covered in animal hides. The third gleamed golden in the sun. I guessed that one was Tut's. Even his horses were decked out as befitted a king—someone had tied ostrich and peacock feathers to the horses' manes and tails, and their backs were covered by bright, multi-colored blankets.

Like I said before, the boy sure loved his bling. Even the wheels of the chariot were trimmed with gold, which, I supposed, was the ancient Egyptian version of rims.

A glance at Grant showed he'd paled under his tan, and I remembered him saying that he was afraid of horses. Even though he'd be riding in a chariot and not actually *on* a horse, he still looked scared.

"Hey," I said softly, grabbing Grant's arm. "It'll be okay. You don't have to actually get on one of the horses. You only need to steer them."

"Have you seen those things? They look dangerous!" Grant said. His eyes looked wild, and I figured that not all of the sweat on his forehead was from the heat. He was really scared. No, beyond scared. Grant was terrified.

"You can't walk, Grant. You have to get on one of the chariots and drive it. How hard can it be? It's not like trying to drive stick or anything. I'll keep close by you, don't worry," I said. I could see I'd surprised him... hell, I surprised *myself*. Since when did I get to be so comforting?

Oh yeah. I remember. Since he kissed me and I want him to do it again, I thought, biting back a smile.

"Oh? Since when are you an expert on chariot driving?" he asked, frowning.

"Since I'm not afraid, and you are."

"I'm not afraid!" he hissed, pulling his arm away from me. "I'm just... cautious."

"Yeah? Well, if you're any more *cautious*, you're going to pee yourself." Tough words, and I hated saying them, but I could see I'd dented his pride, and that was just what he needed. He'd get up on the chariot and drive it even if it killed him, just to prove me wrong. The smile escaped my control, and I grinned.

It wasn't necessary for me to help Grant, since there was a servant for that purpose, and I could see my attention made him a little braver, but when he stepped up into the chariot and took the reins, I could see his hands shaking.

I couldn't decide if Grant looked ready to scream or throw up as a servant showed him how to guide the horse. He fisted the reins so hard that his knuckles turned white.

I was kind of excited to drive a chariot. Then again, I was always ready to try new things, although I admit they weren't always in my best interest. Sometimes they just seemed to be a good idea at the time (for example, me stealing a car to go for a joy ride), but the chariots didn't appear to be self-destructive as far as I could see, and I was anxious to see what they could do. I didn't pay much attention to the horses that were going to pull my rig, but maybe I should have.

One of my horses hated me. I know this for a fact because he kept tossing his head around and kicking out with a hind foot, which made the whole contraption shake violently. I named him "Meek," after the dean, not only because the horse was so surly, but also because they sort of looked alike... well, except for the fact that I thought the Meek at home might weigh more than the horse.

Tut was obviously very familiar with his chariot. He took the reins, flicked them over the horses' backs, and set off at a good clip.

I heard Grant yelp as his horses took off after Tut's, trotting over the desert sand.

My horses stood stock still, and Meek kicked again. No matter how hard I flicked the reins, or clicked my tongue, or swore up a storm, Meek wouldn't move. The other horse tried, but he couldn't go anywhere without Meek's cooperation.

Stupid Meek.

Just when I thought I was going to have get off the chariot and pull it across the desert myself, he launched himself forward. I had to grab tight to the edge of the chariot to keep from being thrown off the damn thing.

Well, that's karma for you, I guess. Here I was worried about Grant, and *I* was the one who nearly ended up butt-first in the sand.

The horses galloped on, and the chariot bumped and jerked, but I managed not to fall off. I have to give the horses this much—they made pretty good time. We caught up to Tut and Grant even though they'd had a head start.

And then we passed them.

I yanked back on the reins, but my horses evidently had missed the day in chariot-training when they were taught how to stop. No matter how hard I pulled back on the reins and shouted "Whoa!" or "Stop, you freaking crazy horses!" they didn't even slow down. We left Tut and Grant and the servants who were walking on foot all in our dust.

By this time, it felt as if my spine was going to pop right out of my mouth from the jarring ride. The ancient Egyptian dune buggy made for a hard ride over the lumpy sand. It felt a little like off-roading in an ATV, except rougher. Luckily, we were nearing the Great Pyramid (although the horses refused to stop or even slow down, they at least seemed to know which way to go, which was lucky for me, because I didn't have clue). I wondered whether they'd stop when we got there, or keep right on going until we ended up splattered against the side of the pyramid like a bug on a windshield.

The hot desert wind blew sand into my face as we raced toward the pyramids. It was a really rough ride; I was worried that one of the wheels might snap off. If I was thrown while the chariot was rolling at such breakneck speed, I'd be in for a world of trouble. There'd be no doubt that I'd get hurt, maybe seriously.

Either Meek had a few more brains than I gave him credit for having, or the other horse decided enough was enough, because they slowed down and eventually stopped when we reached the base of the Great Pyramid of Khufu. I jumped off, and Meek promptly turned his head and tried to bite me.

Well, we were even. I didn't like him anymore than he liked me. "Bite me, and I'll make sure we have horse burgers tonight for dinner," I said, jumping out of the way of his gnashing teeth.

I knew one thing for sure. If we didn't get the amulet before it was time to return to Tut's house in Giza, I wanted a different horse, or I was hoofing it home on my own two feet.

After what seemed like forever, Tut and Grant arrived at the pyramid. The servants would be awhile yet, I figured, since they were hiking on foot.

Grant must've gotten over his fear of his horses, because he was grinning and looking as if he was having the time of his life.

"What was the big rush?" he asked, walking up to me. "You shot by us so fast I thought your horses' butts must've been on fire."

"This one's defective," I sniffed, indicating Meek. "He doesn't have brakes. What have you got to smile about, anyway? I thought you were petrified of riding."

Grant shrugged a shoulder. "It wasn't really *riding*. It was driving, and like I told you before, I was just being cautious. Besides, I don't know what I was so worried about anyway. Once we got going, it was fun!"

Fun. Yeah, it was fun, like a trip to the dentist for a root canal was fun.

At least, for me, anyway.

I forgot about Meek and how much I wished he was glue as Grant and I stood in the shadow of the Great Pyramid. This close, I couldn't see the top, not even craning my neck and leaning backward. It was, I realized, the ancient world's version of a skyscraper. It was at least four hundred and fifty feet tall! I did the math in my head, and realized that worked out to about forty-five stories. No wonder it had been one of the Seven Wonders of the Ancient World. I was willing to bet there wasn't anything manmade on earth that was taller.

It was amazing. I couldn't even begin to imagine how they'd built it without cranes and other heavy machinery. One block alone had to be almost five feet tall, and just as wide, and must've weighed a couple of tons! They got smaller as the rows got higher, but still, we were talking about millions of tons of rock. How had they managed to drag the blocks all the way from the quarry, and pile them up using only sledges and ropes? Yet the stones were set together so tightly, I doubted that I could slip a playing card between them.

Tut walked up to us, chuckling. "To watch you, I would think you never drove a chariot before. Do they not have horses and chariots in your country?" he asked me. "How can you live in such a backward place? I will send some mares and a fine stallion with you when you return home, so that you may breed your own herd. I will send a chariot as well, so that your people may see it and marvel at the greatness of Egypt. Your king will be most impressed."

I was embarrassed that Tut had remarked on my driving ability—or lack thereof—and felt my face grow hot. *Let's see you jump behind the wheel of a Mustang in my world and drive like a pro!* I thought, but tactfully changed the subject. The last thing I wanted was to antagonize Tut, especially when my ticket home was hanging around his neck. "Are you going to have a tomb built like this one? A pyramid?" I asked. I didn't want to talk about Tut's death, not really, but I was embarrassed about my chariot-driving abilities, and the question just popped out.

He shook his head. "No. My tomb lies far to the south in the Valley of the Kings, near Thebes. It will be grand, make no mistake, and filled with all my treasure so that I will have use of my wealth in the next world. For this reason, my tomb must be well hidden from thieves."

I knew no one would find Tut's tomb for over three thousand years, which went to show just *how* secret the location of Tut's tomb would be, but didn't think it was a good idea to say so. I pointed to the Great Pyramid. "Are we going to go inside?"

Tut looked shocked. "No, of course not! The pyramid is sealed. It is the sacred resting place of Khufu. It would be blasphemy to desecrate it by entering! We will go instead to the funerary temple, there," he said, pointing to a walled-in structure adjacent to the pyramid. "I will leave an offering of dates and barley and ask the gods for the proof I require. Come! We will wait in the shade of the temple for my servants to arrive."

Well, I thought with relief, *at least it answers my question about what Tut would leave as an offering.* No human sacrifices here, I was glad to note.

Grant and I exchanged a glance and shrugged at one

another because we both would've liked to see the inside of the Great Pyramid, but followed along behind Tut as he walked toward the opening in the wall that surrounded the temple.

Chapter Fifteen

The inside of the funerary temple was nothing like I'd expected it to be. I thought it would be more like a chapel, with pews and an altar, but it looked very little like any church I'd ever been in. There was a statue inside at the head of the room, that Tut told us was Khufu, himself, in his Divine form. In front of the statue there was a beautifully dyed, woven rug spread on the ground, and a small, empty platter.

That was it.

After seeing the grandeur of the pyramids, I'd figured I'd see the same type of splendor in the temple, with lots of gold and treasure, paintings and hieroglyphics, but it was very plain and simple inside. Tut explained that this place was only for communication between the king or his priests and the gods. It didn't need to be rich or elaborate. The wealth of the king needed to be buried with his body, not used in the temple.

He told us that the Egyptians believed death was only a continuation of life, complete with your original body, all its parts, and all the riches, servants, and status you'd accumulated in life. I thought his version of death sounded like graduating high school and going off to college—you were still you, still in school; you had your same MP3 player and favorite pajama bottoms, but it was a different kind of experience in a different place.

When Tut's servants arrived, he met them outside the temple. No one was supposed to be inside the temple except for his priests or Tut, who, since he claimed he would be a god after his death, was the go-between for his people and the gods while alive. I guess it said a lot about the trust Tut had in Grant and me that he allowed us to be in there at all.

He came back inside with his arms full. He showed us a sack of barley, one of dates, a small basket of incense, a few gold rings, a lion's pelt, and a loaf of bread.

Grant and I hung back and watched as Tut knelt by the colorful rug and placed the items on it. He put the bread and some dates on the platter, and then arranged the other items carefully on the rug before the statue.

Tut knelt before the statue and touched his head to the ground. I realized it was the first time I'd seen Tut lower his head to anyone. It was a gesture of how highly he regarded his ancestor, Khufu, I supposed.

He sat back on his haunches and began to speak. His language was formal and old-fashioned, not the more familiar everyday speech of the Egyptians. "Behold, the Osiris Ani, the scribe of the holy offerings of all the gods, saith: Homage to thee, O thou who hast come as Khepera, Khepera the creator of the gods, Thou art seated on thy throne, thou risest up in the sky, illumining thy mother, Nut, thou art seated on thy throne as the king of the gods."[1]

Tut went on for quite some time. I heard many names mentioned that I halfway recognized—Osiris,

---

1   The Papyrus of Ani (Egyptian Book of the Dead). "A Hymn of Praise to Ra When He Riseth in the Eastern Part of Heaven. "

Isis, Anubis, Khufu, and Tut's father, Akhenaten, among them. "Oh, glorious Ones, I humbly beseech aid. Today, there is a great heartache in Egypt. Nefertiti, Lady of the Two Lands, has disappeared. A cobra may be slithering amongst the People, unseen, seeking to poison the throne of Egypt. I beg Thee grant me the wisdom to know this viper and the strength to crush it beneath my heel, and Thy help to find Thy favored daughter, and deliver her safely home."

I exchanged a look with Grant. Neither of us thought Tut was likely to find Nefertiti alive, but we couldn't bring ourselves to tell him.

Aye was our number one suspect in both Nefertiti's disappearance and in Tut's future murder. Somehow, we had to convince Tut not to trust Aye.

Oh, yeah... and get the amulet. We needed to get it away from Tut, and soon. It was our only ticket home. I know Merlin said time didn't work the same in the present as it did in the past, but I really didn't want to take any chances. It would royally suck to go home and find out I was an old man.

Tut got up and walked back to where we stood. "Come," he said. "We will go back and prepare to travel home to my palace in Memphis. The gods will give me my answer in their own time."

We nodded and followed him outside the temple to where the horses and servants waited. I wasn't looking forward to getting on the chariot behind Meek again, and was trying to convince Grant to switch horses with me, when suddenly Tut froze and pointed toward the south. "Someone comes!" he cried.

Sand swirled on the distant horizon, the sort kicked up by horse's hooves. I squinted, but couldn't make out any figures through the dense cloud. "Who is it?"

"I do not know. Perhaps the Hittites," Tut said. He ran toward his servants, taking his bow and arrows from them. "Arm yourselves with whatever weapons you can find."

Arm myself? As in, grab a weapon and get ready to fight? I was a thief, not a warrior! I turned toward Grant in a panic, but he looked as startled as me. We stared at each other, then at the barren sand around us. "What are we supposed to do? Throw sand in their eyes?" I murmured.

There was a wild look in Grant's eyes as he scurried around, picking up pebbles and rocks from the ground near the base of the temple.

"Grant! By the time you get close enough to chuck one of those rocks, they'll have shot you with so many arrows you'll look like a porcupine," I said, knocking the rocks out of his hands. "We have to get out of here!"

"We can't just leave Tut!" Grant cried. "They'll kill him!"

He had a point. Of course, I didn't want to point out to him that they'd kill us, too, whoever "they" were. "Tut!" I shouted, running up to him. He was standing on the back of his chariot, a carved and polished bow in his hands already fitted with a deadly-looking arrow. "We have to get out of here, or hide! There's only one of you, and who knows how many of them!"

He scowled at me. "You would have me hide like a frightened child? The gods will protect me!"

I could hear them coming, now, a muted thunder of hooves striking the sand. Fear squeezed my chest like a giant fist. This wasn't some goofy re-enactment or play—this was for real. Somebody was going to get hurt or dead, and considering there was only myself, Tut, Grant, and a handful of servants, and Tut was the only one armed, unless you counted the eating knives the servants held, then that somebody was likely to be Grant or me or both. "Tut, be reasonable! You can't fight them all!"

Tut turned back to face the coming horde, his face as stony as the pyramid behind him. Damn him! He was going to get himself killed right in front of me!

I stepped up behind him on the chariot, ready to throw my arms around him and cart his stubborn ass back inside the temple, when the first of the chariots emerged from the dust cloud. Tut lowered his bow, and I squinted over his shoulder.

It was Aye.

My relief was very short-lived. Why had Aye brought what looked like an entire company of archers in chariots if only to fetch Tut back to the palace? What if the anthropologists back home were wrong? What if Tut was murdered when he was seventeen, not nineteen? Two years didn't seem like much of a margin of error when you considered that Tut's mummy was over three thousand years old. What if *today* was the day he died?

I hopped off the back of the chariot and stood next to Grant. "What are we going to do?"

Grant shrugged his shoulders. He looked as worried as I was.

"We have to do something!"

"We don't know what Aye wants, Aston. We have to wait and see," Grant whispered. "If we try anything—and it would be idiotic anyway, since, in case you didn't notice, Aye has a really big sword, and those other men have bows and arrows, while all we have are stupid *rocks*—he'll kill us as sure as we're standing here."

By now, Aye had pulled his chariot to a halt about twenty feet in front of Tut. He stepped down and walked to Tut's chariot. The rest of his men stopped farther back in a long, straight line. That he was furious was plain enough to see—his brows were knit together in a fierce scowl, and his face was beet red, although I suppose he was mindful of both the servants and his men, since he kept his tone respectful. "My Lord, what are you doing out here without an armed guard?"

"Your place is not to question me," Tut answered, returning Aye's frown with one of his own. I was proud of Tut for standing up to Aye and not letting Aye cow him. "Why are you not guarding Memphis? Have you brought me good news? Has Nefertiti been found? Have the Hittites retreated from the borders of Egypt?"

Aye looked torn, as if he wanted to scream at Tut, and he took a minute before answering. "No, my Lord, Nefertiti is still missing, and the Hittites remain camped just outside our border."

"And yet you saw fit to bring an entire company of my best archers up the Nile and across the desert? For what purpose, Aye?" Tut didn't bother to lower his voice, and I could see the archers in the chariot line turn to one another, whispering, no doubt about the king reaming the Grand Vizier a new one.

"Forgive me, my Lord. I was worried for your safety."

I could see it was costing Aye to ask Tut for anything, particularly forgiveness. It looked as if Aye clenched his teeth any harder, they would shatter.

"It is no matter. I am done here now. We will return to Giza, and on the morrow, to Memphis. Take my archers and go back to the city. We will follow shortly," Tut ordered.

"We will travel with you, to protect you," Aye said.

"Do you have sand in your ears, Aye? I said to go back to Memphis immediately, and we will follow at my leisure," Tut said again. His eyes snapped fire as he stared Aye down.

Aye stammered a bit, obviously trying to come up with something that would force Tut to let the archers accompany him. I wondered why he wanted to travel with us so badly.

"The Hittites, my Lord. Should you be attacked—"

Tut raised a hand, cutting Eye off. "Did you not just inform me that the Hittites remained camped outside of Egypt's borders?"

Grant nudged me with an elbow. "This is sacred land," he whispered.

I glanced at the pyramids, and nodded. "Yeah, so?"

"Maybe Aye doesn't want to murder the pharaoh where he believes the gods are watching."

Grant must have been thinking along the same lines as me. His theory explained why Aye wanted to travel with Tut. If Aye wanted to murder Tut, he wouldn't want to do it on sacred ground. Plus, if he did it here, he'd have to kill Tut, us, and Tut's servants, and probably the warriors he'd brought with him, to be sure there were no witnesses. It would just be easier and safer to do it if he was traveling with us, when the servants were walking far behind Tut and couldn't see him, and the archers were preoccupied with watching for danger. He could even blame the murder on Grant and me! No one in Egypt would take our word over Aye's.

But who exactly were these "Hittites" Tut mentioned? Enemies of Egypt, no doubt. It seemed to me that ancient civilizations were always fighting with one another.

I thought briefly about the wars going on in my own time, and figured that nothing had really changed much in three thousand years.

I held my breath, silently praying for Tut to stay strong and to send Aye on his way. We'd have to keep a careful eye out on the way back, just in case Aye planned to ambush Tut, although I didn't think Aye would be that stupid. His archers would wonder why he wasn't accompanying them back to Memphis, and if he kept them with him, it would difficult for him to wait in ambush to kill Tut while his men were watching.

"My Lord, surely you can understand my reluctance to—"

"You try my patience, Aye! Do you seek to embarrass Pharaoh in front of his troops and servants? Or has the time come for you to step down as Grand Vizier?" Tut hissed.

I watched as Aye's face, furiously red just a moment before, paled. "Of course not, my Lord. I am ever a faithful and obedient servant. I have served Egypt and you well, lo, these many years since your father's death."

"Then go. This conversation has reached its end." Tut lifted his chin, staring straight over Aye's head.

Aye turned away, but not before I saw furious anger and hatred in his eyes. If I hadn't been sure before that Aye was the one who'd murdered Tut, I was now.

We watched in silence as Aye ordered the archers to turn, and led them away. It wasn't until the sand kicked up by the horses' hooves on the horizon settled that we began to ready ourselves to leave.

Tut's face was still granite-hard, his body tense. I could tell he was angry, but whether it was because he now suspected Aye of plotting against him, or because his authority had been challenged in front of us, his servants, and the archers, I didn't know. Somehow, I got the feeling that Tut believed the gods had just given him the answer he sought, even if he wouldn't say it out loud.

All I *did* know was that things were heating up in Egypt, and I wanted to snatch the amulet and get home before Grant and I ended up roasting in the fire.

Chapter Sixteen

"This is ridiculous," I said. I'd been pacing back and forth in my small room for what felt like hours, and probably was. If I kept it up, I was going to wear grooves in the rock floor. I'd been on edge ever since we'd gotten back to Memphis from Giza the night before. The look on Aye's face when he'd left us at the pyramids haunted me. I had the feeling things were going to go bad very quickly.

It was morning, but I hadn't slept much. Neither had Grant, and he'd come knocking on my door before dawn.

He sat cross-legged on my bed, watching me. He didn't say anything, but I knew he was as frustrated and worried as me. We had to get out of Egypt, and we were running out of time.

"How can it be so freaking hard to steal one stupid, little piece of jewelry?" I fumed. "It didn't take me this long to figure out how to hot wire a car!" I stopped pacing and looked at him. "And you! You broke into an office building. Why is it you can't sneak into Tut's bedroom? It's not like he has the place wired for alarms."

Grant snorted. "No, he just has a pair of really big guards with really pointy swords standing outside his door. Plus, let's not forget that we were such great thieves that we got *caught*, remember? We don't want to make the same mistakes here. We won't go to juvenile detention if we get caught... we'll go to the cemetery."

I sat down next to him, rubbing my neck as if I could already feel the guard's sword at my throat. "Yeah, don't remind me. So, what do you think we should do?"

"Go swimming."

I blinked and stared at him. "What? You're kidding, right?"

"Nope. Think about it. We know Tut takes his amulet off when he takes a bath. Remember the first night we were here? We saw his servant help him take it off."

"Yeah, so?"

"Well, it stands to reason that he doesn't like to get it wet, or it's too clunky to wear in the water. If we went swimming, he'd probably take it off there, too. We just have to get him to go with us without his servants. While he's with one of us in the water, the other can snatch the amulet." Grant smiled smugly, as if he was convinced he'd thought of the answer to our problem.

"There's just one thing wrong with your plan, oh great genius," I said.

"What? There's nothing wrong with it. It's perfect!"

"Oh, yeah? Have you seen any built-in swimming pools or water parks while we've been here? When Egyptians go swimming, they go into the *river*, remember?"

He raised an eyebrow. "And that's a problem because...?"

I rolled my eyes at him. "The *Nile*? Snakes, crocodiles, hippos? Any of this ringing a bell?"

He huffed and crossed his arms over his chest. "Well, I don't hear any brilliant ideas coming from your direction. We'll be careful, and we don't have to be in the water for long. Just a few minutes would do it. Once we have the amulet, we'll get sucked back to our time."

A new worry etched another wrinkle in my forehead. "We *hope* we'll get sucked back to our time. What if Merlin is wrong, and his magic only works in one direction?" I asked.

Grant's eyes widened "Don't even go there," he cried. I guess he hadn't thought of that possibility either. "It *has* to work! I can't begin to think about being stuck here for the rest of my life!"

"Yeah, me, too. I couldn't stand it! I'd have to throw myself to the crocodiles. All right. We'll give your plan a try."

He seemed to relax, and smiled at me. "Good. When should we talk to Tut?"

"The sooner the better, I guess. After breakfast?"

"Okay." He took a deep breath, then stood up. "Let's go do this thing."

We sat across from each other on Tut's bed, with Tut between us as we ate our usual breakfast of fruit, meat, and bread. I was waiting for Grant to bring up the subject of swimming—it'd been *his* idea, after all—but I guess he was waiting for me to do it. As a result, neither of us said anything. We just stared at each other, trying to give the other the message with our eyes.

"You are too quiet this morning, my friends," Tut finally said, looking first at Grant, then at me. "Did you argue?"

"Huh?" I looked at Tut. "Argue? Nah, we're fine."

Tut reached for another hunk of bread. "Ah. This is good. No argument was ever won by silence," he said. "I sense something is wrong, though. You usually chatter like a pair of monkeys. What is it?"

Grant and I looked at each other again. "Nothing's wrong, it's just that, well, we, uh... we were wondering if you'd want to go swimming with us later, Tut," he said.

"Yeah," I added. "Just the three of us."

Tut cocked his head at us. "Why? If you wish to bathe, I will have the servants attend you."

Damn! "No, that's not it. Um..." My mind raced, trying to come up with an excuse to get Tut alone at the river. "In our country, people often go swimming for fun. You know, just to hang out with their friends and forget their problems for a while."

Grant chimed in. I noticed that his grin was strained. I could practically see every tooth in his mouth. He was trying too hard. "Yeah! It's fun, and it's good to get away for a few minutes. You're under a lot of pressure, Tut."

"Yes, but I am Pharaoh. It is to be expected," Tut replied. "I cannot forget my duties. Nefertiti is still missing, the Hittites remain camped just outside our borders, and Aye..."

"And Aye...?" I prompted. I knew it was right there on the tip of Tut's tongue. I wanted to hear him say it. *Say it,* I thought, trying to project my thoughts into Tut's head. *Say that you don't trust Aye. Then at least I can go home without worrying that you'll just let him walk up to you and kill you.*

Tut shook his head as if to clear it. "It is nothing. You are right. I would enjoy a brief respite. Come, finish eating, and we will walk down to the river," he said.

Damn it! What was it going to take to get Tut to admit that Aye was a threat to him? *Maybe I should just tell Tut,* I thought. *Blurt it right out. Aye is going to kill you,*

Tut. After yesterday, I was sure Tut believed it now. I just wanted to hear him actually say *it.*

I opened my mouth to try again, to say something—anything—that might get Tut to see what was right there in front of him, when suddenly a soldier burst into the room. He was dressed in the standard Egyptian kilt, a white headdress, and wore a scabbard at his hip. He knelt at Tut's feet.

"Forgive me, my Pharaoh. Aye has sent me. General Horemheb has sent word of a Hittite attack."

Tut dropped his glass, unmindful of the milk that spilled over the bed, and jumped to his feet. "An attack? Where?"

"South of here, at a small village They left their campfires burning to fool our scouts and crossed the river under cover of darkness. The Grand Vizier went with the General to inspect the village, and has sent word that everyone there is dead. The Hittites have returned to their camp across the river, but Aye and Horemheb fear more attacks are to come."

"Where is Aye now?" Tut asked. His eyes shone with excitement. "Is my army ready to march?"

"Two regiments await you just outside the city gates, my Pharaoh. The Grand Vizier and General Horemheb wait to the south with the larger portion of your army, near where we must cross the great river to reach the Hittite camp."

"Good. Summon my servants with my weapons and shield, and ready my chariot," Tut ordered. He glanced back at Grant and me. "Outfit my friends with weapons as well. Take them from my personal armory. I'm sure they will not want to miss an opportunity for glory in battle!" he said as he walked away briskly. He never looked back at us again, as if he was certain we would be eager to follow him into combat. He left before either of us could voice an argument.

He said it as if going to war was nothing more than a field trip to an amusement park. Grant and I stared after him with our mouths hanging open. Surely, he didn't mean he expected us to *fight?* We didn't know the first thing about being soldiers, ancient Egyptian or otherwise!

"This is nuts." Grant whispered. He looked every bit as shocked as I felt. "We can't go to war. We're just kids."

"We're adults here," I reminded him. "Besides, if anything happens to Tut, we'll *never* get the amulet! What if he loses it on the battlefield and the enemy finds it? We'd never get it back. We can't risk it. We *have* to go, if for nothing else but to keep him from losing it."

"Yeah? And while we're protecting Tut and the amulet, what's going to keep *us* from getting dead?"

I rolled my eyes, not wanting to seem like a coward, although in truth, I was shaking in my sandals. "We'll be careful. Besides, Tut is the pharaoh. He won't be on the front lines or anything, right? Don't kings stay behind the troops, calling the shots? I mean, our President doesn't actually pick up a machine gun and lead the charge when we're at war, does he?"

Grant didn't look convinced, but he knew what I did. We had to stay close to the amulet, or we'd never get home. "Okay. I suppose you're right. We'll keep our heads low, but whatever you do, don't try to be a hero, okay?"

"Hero? The only 'hero' I know is a sandwich," I said, as a couple of servants entered the room, dragging shields, spears, and knives with them.

The servants, both younger than Grant and me,

expertly outfitted us. They handed us each a shield—a dark brown sheet of heavy leather stretched across a wooden frame—that was nearly as tall as we were. The spears were long, smooth shafts of wood topped with a bronze blade that was easily the length of my hand, and almost as wide at its bottom, narrowing to a wickedly sharp point. The servants strapped sheaths to our waists with leather belts. The sheaths held knives, and when I pulled mine out, I saw that it had a carved ivory handle and a razor-sharp, bronze blade.

Weighted down by the spear, shield, and knife, I felt like I could barely walk, never mind defend myself. The shield especially was big and awkward. It covered me from head to knee, though, so I figured it was a good thing. I only hoped the leather was thick enough to stop an arrow. I didn't plan on getting close enough to anybody to risk getting stabbed with a spear or sword.

News of the attack by Tut's enemies must have traveled like wildfire through Memphis. Crowds of people had gathered at the gates to watch the soldiers waiting outside the city walls get ready to march. They cheered and threw flower petals at the feet of the soldiers.

Grant and I struggled with our equipment as we followed the servants out of the palace to where the chariots (I cringed as I recognized my horse-enemy, Meek) waited. In each chariot, an archer stood.

"Who are those guys?" I asked Grant. Since my hands were full carrying my shield and spear, all I could do was point my chin toward the archer who stood behind Meek.

"Archers."

"Well, no duh. What are they doing in our chariots?"

"Maybe we're walking," Grant mused, looking as confused as I was.

"Oh, swell. Walking through the desert carrying all this crap? I'll be dead before we even reach the Hiccups."

"*Hittites*," Grant growled, rolling his eyes at me. "Pay attention, will you? The least you can do is get the name of the enemy right."

"Wow, *somebody* got up on the wrong side of the pyramid this morning."

"Gee, maybe I'm a little grouchy because we're marching off to *war*, when I *should* be marching off to physics class!" he retorted.

I had to hand it to Grant, he could be quick with a comeback sometimes. "Yeah? Well, here I am marching out along *with* you, but you don't see me biting *your* head off."

He grunted and mumbled an apology, which I accepted with a snort.

We were big on communicating with noises, Grant and me.

A commotion behind us drew our attention from our little spat. Tut had arrived in all his battle regalia. Escorted by eight guards, two on each side, he stalked straight toward his chariot with his chin held high and excitement gleaming in his eyes.

I don't know what I expected him to be wearing—a suit of armor, maybe—but this wasn't it. Tut wore a white linen kilt edged with sparkling gems. He was bare-chested, but wore a necklace that was so wide it practically constituted a shirt. It was made of small, golden scales, studded with jewels, and covered the top part of his chest and back, and both shoulders. Merlin's amulet—Tut's amulet at the moment, I reminded myself—lay on top of it. Gold armbands encircled each of his biceps and ankles. His tall, cone-shaped white hat trimmed with ostrich feathers sat on his head. As he walked past me, I noticed the soles of his sandals had been painted with tiny figures.

"Jeez, did he really need to decorate the bottoms of his shoes?" I whispered to Grant.

"Maybe it's supposed to show that he's walking all over his enemies," Grant offered.

That made sense, in a weird, ancient Egyptian sort of way. Even back here in the B.C. of time, it was all about intimidation and looking impressive—like guys who tattoo their knuckles, or paint flames on the hoods of their cars.

Tut held a shield with one hand, and in the other he carried a wicked-looking short sword that was curved like a scythe. Its bronze blade glittered in the sunlight like the jewels in his collar.

Tut didn't speak to us or even look in our direction as he walked to his chariot and climbed up behind another man. His driver, I guessed. I supposed kings didn't drive themselves when going to battle.

Even his horses were decked out. Someone had again tied ostrich and peacock feathers to their manes and tails, and in addition to the colorful blankets on their backs, there was a sort of golden mask fitted over their faces.

Then I saw other soldiers climbing aboard the chariots behind the archers and taking the reins. Each chariot had two men on it, so I figured we were all riding double today. I nudged Grant, and we headed for our chariots. I jumped aboard the closest one, crowding in close behind the archer, who turned sideways to allow me to reach the reins. That left the chariot Meek was harnessed to for Grant. I grinned at the black look he shot me when he realized which horse was part of the team pulling his rig.

Hey, you snooze, you lose, right? Besides, I'd put up

with Meek enough on the trip to the pyramids. It was Grant's turn to deal with Meek trying to take a bite out of him.

Tut raised his weapon high in the air and gave a shout, and we began to move. Grant and I were close behind Tut. We kept to an arrowhead formation, with Tut's chariot in the lead as we headed south across the desert to where the rest of Tut's army waited.

Chapter Seventeen

Tut's army was camped near the river on a wide expanse of empty land. I supposed I thought there would be a couple of hundred men or so, and I was shocked to see *thousands* of men, a sea of warriors, spread out across the sand. Hundreds of chariots were parked, row after row, on the far right hand side, furthest from the water, the horses turned out to graze.

The noise of so many people and horses was incredible, a constant thrum that resonated in my bones. But it was the smell that surprised me more than anything. I'd been in crowded places before, concerts, theme parks, and county fairs, but this... It was as if someone had taken all the foul smells in the world, put them in a test tube, and stuck it under my nose.

I'd forgotten that we were in a time before deodorant. You know that funky smell gym socks get when they've been sitting forgotten in your locker for a couple of weeks? Combine it with the smells of horses, manure, human waste, smoke, food cooking, and the mucky, fishy smell of the riverbank, bake it all for hours under the broiling desert sun, and that's the stench that hit me squarely in the face when we rode into camp. It was almost enough to make me blow chunks.

I glanced at Grant. He had his arm crooked over his

nose and mouth, so I knew I wasn't alone in gagging on the smell. Somehow, while we'd been in the city where people bathed often and constantly used perfumed oils, flower petals, and candles, it hadn't stunk nearly as badly. Oh, don't get me wrong, there had been places in Memphis that we'd passed by that smelled like ripe armpits, but here in the desert, where thousands of men were sweating buckets, belching, and farting, horses were crapping wherever they felt like it, and meat and fish burned on campfires, it was a complete stink fest.

We left the chariots near the others, where servants were waiting to tend the horses, and followed Tut to a large, white tent set up near the center of the encampment. The roof was peaked, and it had steeply sloped sides, and two guards stood sentry by the entrance. Both Grant and I had to duck to enter through the front flap.

Inside, large pillows covered the sand, and two servants stood ready to tend to Tut's needs. He looked tired as he sank onto the pillows and motioned for us to join him. "Food and water," he ordered, sending the servants scrambling out of the tent to secure both for him. They returned quickly, pouring water for all of us and placing a large platter of meat and fruit in front of Tut.

Inside the shade of the tent, it had to be a whole quarter of a degree cooler than it was outside, but at least it didn't smell as bad. I noticed there were tall stands set at all four corners of the tent that held bowls of sweet-smelling herbs and burning incense. They helped keep the air inside the tent relatively stench-free, for which I could've kissed the servants.

Word that Tut had arrived at the camp must've spread quickly. We didn't have long to wait before Aye entered the tent. He looked angry when he saw Grant and me, but didn't say anything to us. I knew he didn't like us much, considering that we were outsiders and yet had quickly become Tut's friends. He probably didn't trust us.

Aye was right about that. Trusting us would've been a mistake on his part. I was still determined to do everything in my power to keep him from murdering Tut after we got the amulet and went home. I didn't like Aye any more than he liked me.

He sneered at Grant and me, and faced Tut. "My Lord, I must speak with you."

"Speak, Aye," Tut said, after taking a long drink of water. He selected a thick slice of meat and motioned for us to help ourselves.

"Privately, my Lord. What I have to say is for your ears only," Aye insisted.

"Speak or hold your tongue, it is your choice," Tut snapped. "I have traveled all day and am weary. I have no patience for secrecy where none is needed. My friends know of the Hittite attack already."

If looks could kill, Grant and I would've been worm food. Aye shot us a look brimming with hatred, although he kept a respectful tone when he spoke to Tut. "As you please, my Lord. It has been suggested by our spies that the Hittites sent men into Memphis to take Nefertiti," he said. "I fear her dead, my Lord."

Bull, I thought, but kept my mouth shut. Strangers might've been able to get inside Tut's palace—after all, Grant and I had, and easily—but how could they get past Nefertiti's guards and into her bedroom, and then smuggle her out without anyone noticing? It was clear to me that it was an inside job, and I felt sure it had Aye's name written all over it.

"Of course, I sent men across the river as soon as I

received the news. They slaughtered many Hittites in Nefertiti's name. Her honor is restored and her death avenged," Aye said, puffing out his chest proudly. The hatred gleaming in his eyes was unmistakable, although I couldn't decide if it was for Egypt's enemies, or for Tut.

Tut quirked an eyebrow. "What of the attack on our village?"

I already knew what Aye was going to say before he said it.

"The Hittites launched the attack on the village before sunrise and razed it to the ground, my Lord. Our scouts were watching the Hittite campfires. None were extinguished, and we had no idea that the Hittites would dare cross the Nile under the cover of night. None in the village survived. The souls of the dead cry out for vengeance! We must march at daybreak and fight until the sands run red with their foul blood!" Aye replied.

I exchanged a meaningful look with Grant. It was Aye's order to attack the Hittites—probably for no other reason than to strengthen his lie that the Hittites had taken and killed Nefertiti—that had caused the Hittites to counterattack. As far as Grant and I were concerned, the blood of everyone in that village was on Aye's hands.

If I didn't like or trust Aye before, I sure as heck didn't now. What sort of a-hole allowed his own people to be massacred to cover his own treachery?

Tut, however, either didn't or couldn't see through Aye's lies, or didn't care. Maybe he hated the Hittites so much that he *wanted* to believed what Aye claimed was true. I suppose it's easier to put the blame on your enemy than on someone who you thought was your friend.

He nodded in agreement with Aye. "Yes, that is a good plan, indeed. At dawn, I want the infantry ready to cross the river, followed by the charioteers and archers. We will leave no Hittite alive between the riverbank and their camp. If Nefertiti lives, I want her found. If she is dead, I want her body returned for mummification and burial as befitting a queen of Egypt."

Aye bowed and spun on his sandals, stalking out of the tent without another look at Grant or me. I didn't miss the smug look on his face. What a jerk! What sort of guy would be willing to not only wipe out the enemy but his own *people* to cover his butt?

The kind that would be willing to kill his king to get his greedy hands on the throne, that's who, I silently answered myself.

I drank some water, but my appetite was gone. "Where will you be tomorrow, Tut? Here? Or do you set up a command center somewhere else?"

Tut looked confused. "Command center? What is this? Another You-Ess custom?" He shrugged. "It matters not. I will be where I should be—leading my troops into battle. The enemy shall fall to my scimitar and be trampled under the wheels of my chariot! The world will know that the gods ride with me!"

I locked eyes with Grant, feeling the blood drain from my face. Tut was going into battle? How were we supposed to protect him and the amulet now?

I could see Grant was as clueless as I was. He gave a tiny shake of his head, and I knew he meant for me to drop the subject before Tut caught on that we had no intention of fighting. I mean, this wasn't our war, right? We weren't even old enough to fight for our *own* country, let alone a pharaoh who'd been dead for three thousand years!

Again the question rose in my mind: if I died in the

past, would I revert instantly back to my own time, or would I remain dead forever? Would it be as if I were never born in the future?

But Merlin said we couldn't change the past. Wouldn't my dying here do just that? Or would my death count only in changing the future? Was there a difference?

I had no idea and no intention at all of finding out.

"The hour grows late, my friends. Go find your rest, and I will do the same. We must be fresh for the morning battle!" Tut said, dismissing us. His servants instantly closed in, preparing to ready him for bed.

Grant and I left Tut's tent with no real idea of where to go. Grant grabbed my elbow and led me away toward the far side of the camp. All around us, men sat staring quietly into the campfires or sleeping, stretched out on the sand. We wove our way carefully between them, not wanting to draw attention to ourselves.

Finally, we reached the perimeter of the camp, where we found a little privacy behind a couple of palm trees. We sank down to the sand and looked at one another. I shivered a little in the cool desert night air.

"Now what do we do?" Grant asked me. "Tut plans on fighting tomorrow, not sitting back giving orders. We can't do this, Aston! We're not warriors. I don't know the first thing about fighting!"

"Me, either." I frowned, trying to think of a way out of the mess we'd found ourselves in. What would I do if I was in my own time and needed to keep somebody from doing something stupid?

Then it came to me.

If I wanted to keep a friend from going out to fight somebody and maybe getting killed, and he wouldn't listen to reason, I'd do something to make sure he couldn't get to wherever he was going.

I'd give him a flat tire.

My head swiveled to look at the area where the chariots were parked. Tut's was easy to spot—it was the only one trimmed with gold. Even in the moonlight, it glittered.

Chariots, of course, didn't have tires, but they did have wheels... wheels that could be removed.

I was grinning when I turned back to Grant. "Come on, I've got an idea," I said. "You need to cover me and make sure nobody can see what I'm doing."

Grant narrowed his eyes at me. "What are you going to do?"

"Mess with Tut's transportation. If he doesn't have his chariot, he can't go into battle, right?"

A slow smile stretched across Grant's face. "Genius. Pure genius."

"I have my moments," I said, returning his smile. "Let's go. We have to make this quick."

We kept to the darkest shadows at the perimeter of camp as we ran, keeping our heads low, toward Tut's chariot. I felt a little like Tom Cruise in *Mission Impossible*, and fought the urge to hum the theme song.

Slipping behind the chariot so that it would hide us from anyone in camp who might glance in our direction, I studied the wheel. It was made of wood, with metal, probably bronze, covering the spokes, and gold decorations. A thin strip of metal encircled the wheel, like a flat tire. I took out the knife I'd been given and used the blade to saw through the hardened leather thongs that bound the spokes to the wheel, then pushed hard until the spokes broke free.

I wasn't satisfied yet, though. I worked the edge of

my knife between the joints of the chariot frame until I succeeded in prying the wheel itself loose. Bracing my feet against the chariot, I pulled on the wheel with all of my strength. There was a sharp crack, and I winced, afraid that someone might have heard it. Then the wheel came off the axle, and I fell backward.

"Are you okay?" Grant whispered as he helped heave the wheel off of me.

I sat up, feeling my chest, checking for damage. "I'll live," I whispered back. "Think anybody heard that?"

He peered cautiously around the side of the chariot, which now listed sharply toward us, the axle resting on the sand. "I don't think so. I don't see anyone coming."

"Good. Let's get out of here."

We ran in a crouch, again sticking to the shadows and out of range of the firelight, until we reached the far side of Tut's tent. "That should do it," I said. "That chariot isn't going anywhere tomorrow."

Satisfied that we'd prevented Tut from riding off to his doom the next day, we lay down on the sand and tried to get comfortable, but it was easier said than done. The sand made for a lumpy bed, and it was chilly without any blankets. While the desert was broiling hot during the day, at night it cooled off considerably.

I lay on my side with my arm cushioning my head, shivering. Suddenly, I felt a warm body curl up next to me. Looking over my shoulder, I saw Grant smiling sheepishly at me. "Dude, what are you doing?"

He gave a little shrug. "Sharing our body heat. I'm freezing."

His body was curled against my back, and it was doing naughty things to my front. "I don't think this is such a good idea, Grant."

"Why not? It's what the Boy Scouts teach you to do to survive in the wild if you don't have a tent."

I bit back a moan and rolled to my stomach. At least that way, he couldn't see that I was pitching my own personal tent in my kilt. Turning my head, I found myself looking into his eyes. They looked black in the near darkness. His face was in shadow, and I couldn't tell what he was thinking from his expression.

I don't know if he moved forward, or I did, or both of us at the same time, but our lips touched. Did you ever touch a battery with the tip of your tongue and feel a tiny electrical spark? That was how the kiss felt, tingly and warm. It was the sort of kiss that had haunted my dreams, not at all like the bruising one we'd shared back in Tut's palace. My body jumped to attention, as if our lips were playing reveille to the troops.

A small voice spoke inside my head, telling me to back off. Neither of us was ready for anything more than a simple kiss; certainly not on the eve of battle in the middle of ancient Egypt.

I don't think either of us wanted it to end, but we had to breathe eventually, and besides, I knew the voice in my head was right. This could only end badly if we kept going and let nature take its course. I pulled away, lifted myself up on one elbow, and cupped his chin with my free hand. His stubble tickled my palm. "Nice," I whispered. "Did you mean it this time?"

"Yeah, I did, and I have news for you—I meant it the last time, too," Grant said. I could see the whiteness of his teeth glinting in a smile.

"Really? You're not going to go all jackass-y on me in the morning, are you? Blame it on stress? Not going to try beating my head in with a rock, or throwing me in front of a speeding chariot?"

"Nope. Scout's honor." He held up his hand with the Scout's three-finger salute in front of my eyes.

I smiled, too. "Okay, then. Cool." We stared at each other for a long few minutes. I wanted to kiss him again. Oh, God, did I ever, but I knew if I started, I wouldn't want to stop. I sighed, long and deep, then flicked his nose with my fingers.

"Ow! Hey, what're you—"

"Get some sleep, lover boy. I have the feeling tomorrow's going to be a long, crappy day." I scooted away a few inches, rolled to my back, and closed my eyes. I pretended not to notice when he laid his head on my shoulder, but it was difficult.

Really, *really* difficult.

I didn't get much sleep that night. I spent a long time listening to Grant's soft snores and concentrating on keeping my hands to myself. My mind was whirling out of control. Everything was different now, and I had no clue how to handle it.

Our relationship had changed so much in the past few days. It sort of boggled my mind. I mean, we were in the fix we were in because we'd been fighting, trying to knock each other brainless. Then, once we were in Egypt, we became friends out of necessity, since we only had each other to depend on. And now...

What, exactly, *were* we now? Boyfriends? I admitted that I kind of liked the sound of it. *I'd like you to meet my boyfriend, Grant.* Yeah, I liked that a lot. I liked the idea of spending time with him and kissing him whenever I wanted to.

Trouble was, I didn't know if *Grant* would like it once we were home again. *Now* he did, sure, because we were stuck in a world where nobody really knew us, and we only had each other to rely on, but how would he feel once we were back at school? When people would look cross-eyed at us for being more than just friends, and when the name-calling started? Heck, neither of us was "out." Would he want to stay in the closet and keep our being together a secret?

Would I?

I finally decided I just couldn't decide. There was nothing I could do about it now, anyway, not until we scored Tut's amulet and got back home. Until then, I needed to concentrate on getting the amulet, making sure Tut didn't get murdered, and keeping both Grant and me safe. I figured that was more than enough to keep me occupied.

And when we finally *did* get home, well, we'd see what was what then. That was the best I could do.

Chapter Eighteen

The camp woke before the sun. It was still dark when the men began moving around, eating cold breakfasts made from last night's leftovers. I groggily blinked awake and shook Grant's shoulder.

"Hey, get up! It's morning... or it will be soon," I said. He tried to roll over, so I gave him another shake.

He swatted my hand away and slowly sat up, rubbing his face. "Okay, okay. I'm up, I'm up."

Suddenly, a shout went up from the vicinity of the chariots, fully waking both of us instantly. We knew what it was—someone had discovered Tut's chariot had been tampered with during the night. Grant and I looked at each other and held our breaths. Would our plan to stop Tut from going into battle work?

"Okay," I whispered. "Game faces on. We can't let on to Tut that we know anything about what happened to his chariot."

"Well, no *duh*," he said, rolling his eyes at me.

I arched an eyebrow and made a mental note. Boyfriend or not, the sarcasm had to go.

After we'd used the facilities (in this case, a bush near the edge of the camp), we tied on our sheaths, picked up our shields and spears, and hightailed it over to Tut's tent.

"I know not who may have done this, my Lord,"

Aye was saying as we peeked through the flap of Tut's tent. Damn! Aye was the last person I wanted to see that morning.

Tut saw us before we could duck back out, and waved us inside. "Someone has sabotaged my chariot!" he exclaimed. "Surely none of my men would do such a thing, but how could the Hittites have slipped by the guards at the river? I fear it is a sign from the gods, a bad omen. Perhaps they do not wish us to battle the Hittites today."

Aye glanced at us, and his face crumpled into an awful scowl as he pointed a finger at Grant and me. "Perhaps there are traitors among us, my Lord. These two... how well do you really know them? They appeared only a few days ago. Since then, all manner of disasters have befallen Egypt. First Nefertiti was taken, then the Hittites' attack on the village, and now this."

Just as I suspected, Aye was trying to blame Grant and me for everything he'd done! Well, everything except for the chariot... that was our doing, not that I was about to confess. "We had nothing to do with any of that, Tut," I retorted. "First of all, the guards would've told you if we were anywhere near Nefertiti's room that night. Secondly, the Hittites probably wouldn't have raided the village if Aye hadn't gone and attacked them first!"

Aye looked positively furious at my outburst. His face turned scarlet and then purple, and his hand reached for his sword. "How dare you speak of me that way to the pharaoh? I will—"

"You will do nothing," Tut hissed. "Except find out who destroyed my chariot."

I decided to press my luck. "You asked the gods for a sign, Tut. Maybe this is it."

"Sign? What sign?" Aye demanded.

"It is none of your concern. I do not believe our visitors from the You Ess have caused us harm, Aye, but someone has. I order you to find out who is responsible immediately!" Tut barked. "Now! Go!"

For a minute it looked as if Aye might disobey Tut and kill us anyway, but at last he grunted and stalked out of the tent in a huff.

One thing was clear—we'd just made a really bad enemy.

"The sooner we get out of Oz altogether, the safer we'll sleep, m'dear," Grant whispered, quoting a scene from *The Wizard of Oz*.

Unfortunately, our ruby slippers were hanging around Tut's neck.

Tut's ears were sharp. "Oz? What is this 'Oz' you speak of?"

"Nothing, nothing. So, somebody messed with your ride, huh?" I quickly asked. The last thing I wanted to do at the moment was try to explain Dorothy and friends to somebody who'd never seen a photograph, let alone a movie.

"My ride? Do you mean my chariot? Yes," Tut answered, frowning. "I shall have their hands cut off for this."

Ouch. I noticed Grant slip his hands behind his back. I didn't blame him. The thought of having my hands chopped off made me slightly sick to my stomach. I swallowed hard and tried not to look guilty. "So, I guess this means you can't go into battle, huh? Gee, that's a shame. Well, I'm sure Aye can handle it," I said.

"Nonsense. Although I prefer my own, any chariot will do. My men will simply harness my horses to another chariot," Tut said, waving his hand as if it was really not a big deal.

Crap! I looked at Grant, and he seemed just as disappointed as I was. After all the trouble we'd been through, not to mention the risk we'd taken, we hadn't succeeded in stopping Tut from going into battle at all! Now, what were we going to do?

The next thing Tut said made my slightly sour stomach go on full red alert, lurching violently. "You have planted seeds of doubt in my mind about Aye. He dares too much; I no longer trust him at my back. You, my friends, will fight at my side today. Go now, and ready your chariots. We will cross the river as the sun rises."

If I hadn't been so petrified, I would've felt relieved at hearing Tut finally say that he didn't trust Aye. As it was, my heart was pounding.

Oh... oh, *hell*, no. We couldn't go to battle! We could barely drive the damn chariots, never mind try to fight while the things were rocketing over the sand. We'd be killed for sure. "Uh, Tut, I mean, we..." I stammered as my mind raced, trying to find a reason to back out without either angering Tut or making him think we were cowards.

Grant tried, too, but Tut was impatient and cut him off, shooting us a stern look. "You must go *now*. I will follow shortly."

We saw his guards take a small step forward, and knew it was our cue to hightail it out of Tut's tent before he lost patience with us altogether.

Outside the tent, Grant and I paused, staring at each other. "Now, what do we do?" he asked. "Hide?"

The sky to the east was beginning to lighten with the coming sunrise. Men were harnessing the horses to the chariots, while others, the infantry, were already crossing the riverbank. We were out of time.

I gestured around me. "Hide? *Where?* We're in the desert. There's not a lot of coverage here, in case you hadn't noticed."

"You don't have to be sarcastic!" he whispered hoarsely. "I have eyes, you know."

"Sorry. I'm a little nervous, seeing how we're going to have to fight a freaking war!" I retorted.

"Hey, I'm in the same boat you're in, remember? I'm not usually a confrontational type of person. I didn't even like to play dodge ball in gym class!"

"Hey, you two!" a gruff voice called out. "Your chariots are ready. Lord Pharaoh wishes you to ride out to the river with him."

We turned to find two chariots hitched and ready to roll. Meek danced on his toes in front of one of them.

Grant and I made bug eyes at each other, but slowly made our way to the chariots. I think both of us were racking our brains, trying to figure a way out of the mess we'd gotten ourselves into, but neither of us seemed to have any answers. I stepped toward the second chariot, but Grant ran around me and tagged it.

"Oh, no. I had Meek the last time," he said, jumping behind the second team of horses. "He's all yours this time."

"Aw, man, it's going to be bad enough trying to keep my head on my shoulders where it belongs without worrying about Meek taking a chunk out of me besides," I grumbled. I eyed Meek as I walked around the chariot. "You behave, or else you're croc bait, horse," I said to him.

Meek snorted and tried to bite me as I passed. Damn

horse. I dodged him and climbed up into the rig. "If there's one thing I'm not going to miss about this place," I said, picking up the reins, "it's *you*."

Grant was having trouble balancing the reins and his spear and shield all at the same time. "How do they *do* this without dropping everything?" he grumbled.

Beats me, I thought, looking around at the other drivers. The first thing I realized was that nobody rode double into battle. Only the archers were in the chariots, and each man rode alone. The second thing I noticed was how they were managing to guide their horse *and* leave their hands free for their weapons. "Oh, you've got to be kidding me!" I said. "Look at these guys!"

"There's no way! I can't do that," Grant gasped.

"Me, either!" I agreed.

The archers had tied the reins around their bodies, leaving their hands free to use their bows and arrows. By throwing their weight one way or the other, they guided the horses in the direction the archer wanted to go. Leaning backward brought the chariot to a stop, and leaning forward told the horses to get moving. It was amazing to watch, but there was no way I could duplicate their feat. The Egyptians were incredible. Then again, they'd probably learned to drive a chariot at the same age *I* was learning to ride a bike.

Tut appeared from inside his tent. He wore his familiar cone-shaped hat with its bobbing ostrich feathers. The Eye of Ra amulet hung from his neck, and he wore a long shirt of golden, overlapping scales that I figured was some sort of chainmail—the ancient Egyptian answer to the bullet proof vest. I swore I could hear him clinking as he hopped into a nearby chariot. His horses were still wearing their ostrich feathers, colorful blankets, and golden face masks. The chariot was plain and simple, like the rest of ours, but that was where the similarity ended. I realized that anyone who saw him would know he was the pharaoh.

I didn't understand it. "Why does he want everyone to know who he is? Doesn't that make him, like, a prime target or something?" I asked Grant.

"Yeah, but I think the point is for intimidation. He thinks he's a god, remember? If you believed that sort of stuff, then wouldn't you be peeing your pants to see an honest-to-God *god* riding at you?" he answered.

It made sense, I supposed, in an ancient Egyptian sort of way. "What are we going to do?"

Grant didn't have the opportunity to answer. When Tut's chariot pulled away, our stupid horses (okay, maybe they were a lot smarter than I'd like to give them credit for being, since they knew *exactly* what they were supposed to do without our even jiggling the reins) took off after him.

Suddenly, we were surrounded by chariots, all moving toward the riverbank. I saw that the infantry had already crossed the river and was marching double-time in neat lines on the other side.

We were completely boxed in. Tut was directly ahead of us, and the rest of his army on each side and behind us. There was nowhere for us to go but forward. Our horses pulled against the reins, and our chariots rumbled toward the river.

Like it or not, it looked as though Grant and I were going to war.

Chapter Nineteen

I'd thought the Hittites were camped just on the other side of the river, but I was wrong. Tut's army marched for hours toward the rising sun, to the far eastern borders of Egypt. The sun was nearly overhead when I heard a low, droning sound that reminded me of a beehive I'd seen once. We crested a dune and saw the Hittite camp far in the distance. Smoke from their fires curled into the new morning sky. Closer was line after line of Hittite warriors, all facing us. Their own scouts must've seen Tut's army approaching, and they were ready for battle.

Tut's infantry stood in long lines halfway between us and the Hittite army. I saw Tut raise his scimitar to the sky and scream out a war cry that chilled my blood.

Tut's cry was drowned out by the voices of a thousand men answering his call. The infantry, already far ahead of the archers and chariots, broke into a run. Soon all I could see of them was a cloud of dust kicked up by their feet in the distance.

Tut's horses broke into a gallop, which must've been the signal the archers were waiting for, because the horses behind and to the side of us began to run. My horses and Grant's joined the stampede, hurtling themselves forward against their braces. Our chariots rocketed over the sand, bumping, jerking, and jolting. My teeth rattled together from the bone-jarring ride.

The noise grew in volume as we neared the area where the Egyptian and Hittite infantries had met head on. It was horrible mix of metallic clangs as sword met sword, mixed with war cries and the agonized screams of men and horses.

I could smell blood on the hot desert wind. The metallic stench of it filled my nose; it was so strong I could almost *taste* it, like when you get a bloody nose and the blood slides down your throat.

Grant was on my right, his chariot nearly even with mine as we crested another dune. Before us was spread a scene that could've been taken straight out of the movies, except I knew there were no special effects here, no CGI. Every drop of blood was real, and every one of the hundreds of bodies that lay broken on the sands had once been a living, breathing human being.

If I hadn't been scared before, I was now. I could hear my blood pounding in my ears, and the hands that held my reins shook.

Thousands of men fought with swords and spears. The Hittites had chariots, too, but theirs were bigger and heavier than the Egyptians', and each was pulled by four horses. I could see many of them bogged down in the softer sand. They were also clumsy; they tried to wheel and turn, but couldn't do it very quickly. They were powerful, though, and the ones that didn't get stuck in the sand plowed through Tut's infantry like rocks through paper, mowing men down and trampling them under sharp hooves and wooden wheels.

Tut's chariot plunged right into the thick of the battle, dragging Grant's and my chariots with him. I was busy trying to steer my horses around the bodies and away from the charging Hittite chariots, but I saw Tut's scythe flash bronze in the sunlight, slashing at the enemy.

I lost sight of Grant. The Hittites had forced him off to the right, separating us. I jerked the reins hard to the right, and the horses turned, racing across the battle line toward where I'd last seen him. "Grant! Grant!" I screamed, knowing my voice couldn't possibly be heard over the thunderous noise of the battle.

The feet of the armies and the horses kicked up the sand; it was flung by the wind into my face, scraping my skin raw like sandpaper. It bit into my eyes, making them hurt and tear up, until everything looked blurry.

A Hittite chariot closed in on my left, driven by a man with black hair and wild eyes. A second man stood with him on the chariot, holding a sword. Before I could maneuver my chariot away, the second man's sword flashed toward me.

It was probably only instinct that made me raise my shield. I certainly didn't intentionally block the shot, but it worked. The sword bit deeply into the shield, slashing it neatly down the center, but I didn't get so much as a scratch, although I felt the blow travel painfully up my arm into my shoulder.

I heard a voice screaming loudly, and it was only after my horses pulled my chariot away from the Hittite's that I realized it was coming from my own mouth. I screamed myself hoarse, until my voice sounded as rough as the sand that blew all around me.

That was the moment it really sunk into my brain. This wasn't a game. It wasn't a play, or a movie, or bunch of guys re-enacting an old battle. It was real. Men were dying all around me. Some of them weren't even as old as I was, barely more than kids themselves. Their screams of pain rang in my ears. I heard them calling for the gods, for their wives, their children, and their mothers, crying in pain, and calling for help that never came.

What had Grant and I been thinking? This was stupid; no, more than stupid—it was insane! We didn't belong here. We should be back at the Stanton School, going to class and slacking off on our homework! Where *was* Grant? I pictured him dead, crushed under his overturned chariot or hacked into pieces by the Hittites.

I finally spotted him off to the right, his chariot racing toward me. I felt an enormous wave of relief at the sight of him, particularly since he looked okay and still had all his body parts. I pulled hard on the reins, slowing my horses to a walk. When he got closer, I read my name on his lips, although I couldn't hear him over the noise all around us.

He was pointing behind me. I twisted my head, squinting to see through the flying sand.

I knew immediately what Grant was pointing at. It was Tut, and he was in trouble. His chariot had stopped moving; one of his horses was dead. It had fallen to the ground, tipping the chariot precariously to one side. He was surrounded by Hittites, and although he was striking out with his scythe, he couldn't fight them all off for long.

Where were his guards? Where was Aye? Did Aye know Tut was in trouble and think to let the Hittites kill Tut for him? Was that his plan all along? Was that why he'd taken Nefertiti and attacked the Hittite camp to begin with? Was it all a set-up? Did the scientists get Tut's age wrong after all? Did he die, not when he was nineteen, but seventeen? Was today the day?

Not if I could help it.

All these thoughts raced through my mind, but my

body was acting on autopilot. Without even realizing I was doing it, I turned the horses and raced toward Tut. My spear was too long for me to wield while trying to drive the horses, so I slipped my knife out of its sheath. It felt heavy in my hand, but my fingers closed around the ivory handle hard enough to ache.

My horses reached the crowd of men gathered around Tut's chariot, their sharp hooves knocking men this way and that. I didn't look to see if any of the men who fell were hurt or dead; my only concern was getting to Tut.

A sword flashed toward me and I slammed my knife into the arm that wielded it, down to the hilt. I pulled it out, and the man fell away from my chariot, blood spraying from his injured arm.

It was the first time I'd ever intentionally hurt another human being, but that thought didn't register on me until much later. Oh, I wasn't a wuss—I'd been in fights before, sure. A punch here, or shove there, but it had never been anything serious. Not like this, at any rate. At the moment, though, all I knew was fury and fear, and all I could see was an opening that led to Tut. I steered the horses into it and pulled up alongside Tut's chariot. "Get in!" I yelled, swiping to the left and right with my knife, not even counting how many times the blade met with flesh.

Tut hopped quickly from his chariot to mine, crowding in close behind me. Heck, we'd ridden double in a chariot before; I saw no reason why we couldn't do it again. "To the front line!" he cried.

"Hell, no!" I screamed back. "I'm getting you out of here!"

"I must fight!"

"You did! Your men can finish this for you!" I argued.

I yanked on the reins and the horses wheeled, racing back toward Grant's chariot.

All around us, the Egyptian army was cutting through the Hittites like an electric razor buzzes though hair. The Hittites' heavier chariots weren't made for the soft sand of the Sahara. They got stuck often and couldn't maneuver as easily. The Egyptian's lighter chariots were remarkable; it looked almost as if they were surfing the sand, wheeling and turning easily.

Some of the Egyptian chariots had problems, too. Some of them lost wheels, and some hit slopes in the sand that threw the rider, but for the most part, they handled the sand well. There were men on foot racing behind the chariots, taking out the Hittites missed by the archers. I felt sure the battle would soon be over, and the Egyptians would come out on top.

My chariot was closing in on Grant when I felt a blow to my arm. It hurt badly, burning and aching, and I nearly dropped the reins. Still, I was so hopped up on adrenaline that it didn't slow me down. I kept snapping the reins, urging the horses forward at full gallop until I reached Grant, then on toward the river.

Grant's chariot kept pace with mine, and we splashed into the river at the same time. It was only when we were safely on the other side, and I saw Tut's servants racing to meet us, that I pulled the horses to a stop.

I looked down at my arm and saw that it was covered in blood, with the feathered butt of the arrow sticking out of it.

The last things I saw as blackness began to cloud my vision were Grant's horrified expression and the amulet around Tut's neck, twinkling in the sunshine.

Chapter Twenty

I never saw the archers return with the news that the battle had been won, and Tut was victorious. The last thing I remembered was lying inside Tut's tent, waiting for his physicians to remove the arrow from my arm. I don't remember any of the procedure, since they'd fed me some bitter liquid that made me sleep—one of the few lucky breaks I'd gotten since landing my butt in ancient Egypt, I suppose. Grant said it was pretty nasty from start to finish.

He told me later that the arrow had hit bone and hadn't gone all the way through. The physicians had to chop off the feathered butt of the arrow, and then push the arrowhead out through the front. Sure enough, when I woke up, I had fresh wounds on both sides of my arm. It was bandaged with linen, but blood seeped from the holes and marked where my wounds were.

It hurt pretty badly, but I figured I'd live. I could move all my fingers and my wrist, and knew I was lucky that the arrow hadn't broken my arm. I felt a little feverish, though, and was worried about infection, since I knew the Egyptian physicians didn't have access to antibiotics. Wouldn't it just suck to have lived through a battle and getting shot by an arrow, only to die from an infection?

"Hey, you're supposed to be resting," Grant said when

I finally woke, sat up, and looked around. He was sitting on the floor nearby.

I blinked in surprise. We were in my room in Tut's palace! There was the window overlooking the garden, and the cheetah table I'd admired. "How long have I been asleep?" I asked, confused. The last thing I remembered was crossing the river to the camp from the battle, and lying inside Tut's tent.

"Almost two days. Whatever they gave you to knock you out sure did the trick. You've been snoring since they took the arrow out of your arm," Grant said. "How do you feel?"

"Like I was shot by an arrow."

Grant frowned at me. "That's *so* not funny. You scared the crap out of me, Aston. What were you thinking? You could've been killed!"

"Well, maybe it wasn't the most brilliant idea I ever had, but all I could think of was that if the Hittites killed Tut, we'd never get the amulet, and we'd never get home," I said. "Besides, I'm a hero!"

"You were almost a *dead* hero. I swear to God, if you ever do anything so stupid again, I'll kill you myself!" Grant retorted. His eyes were snapping fire, and I could see how upset he was.

"Why, you keep talking like that and somebody might think you actually care about me," I teased, grinning at him.

He turned red and sniffed. "Oh, shut up. I just don't want to have to explain to Merlin why I had to leave your sorry dead butt in Egypt."

A servant came into the room and bowed before us. "Pharaoh wishes to see the young masters," he said. "He waits in the Great Hall."

"I'll go. You need to rest," Grant said, getting to his feet.

"No, I'm fine. I'll go, too," I protested.

"Aston, I don't think—"

"It's just my arm, Grant. I'll be okay." Sheesh. He could be a real mother hen when he wanted to be.

I stood up and swayed a little as the blood rushed to my head, and pain washed through me. Grant took my good arm to steady me. "Oh, yeah, you're fine, all right," he said sarcastically.

"I *am* fine. I just got up too fast," I insisted. My cheeks burned because I was a little embarrassed. I wanted him to see me as a hero, not as a wimp who fainted because of a little scratch on the arm.

Not that it *was* a little scratch. *I was shot by an arrow*, I reminded myself. Still, feeling woozy detracted from my tough-guy image.

"Jeez, you're stubborn as well as stupid," Grant said with a sigh. "Come on, I'll help you. You'll only try to get there on your own if I leave you here."

"Damn straight," I said. I'd tough it out. Besides, I liked feeling Grant's hand on my arm, and liked more the look of concern in his eyes. It didn't matter that he'd called me stupid. The truth was that he was worried about me, and he wouldn't be worried if he didn't care about me.

That thought put a smile on my face despite the pain in my arm. I remembered panicking when I couldn't find him during the battle, and the relief I'd felt when I finally saw him, and knew he was all right. I realized I didn't just like Grant—I cared about *him*, too.

Boyfriends, I thought, smiling. *Yup. Definitely, boyfriends.*

"What are you grinning about?" Grant asked, cocking an eyebrow.

"Oh, nothing," I said. I tried, but I couldn't stop smiling, even though my arm hurt.

We made our way slowly to the Great Hall. Grant refused to let me walk faster than a snail's pace. "Shut up," he said when I complained. "If you pass out, who's going to have to lug your heavy butt back to the bedroom? Me, that's who."

"I'm not going to pass out."

"You lost a lot of blood," he said. "And they don't do transfusions in ancient Egypt."

I wondered exactly *how* much was "a lot." Maybe that was why I felt so weak and shaky, and not just because of the pain. The thought made me feel a little better. "Okay. Slow it is."

Slow it *was*, too. It took us a full ten minutes to walk down the hall, navigate the stairs, and wind our way to the Great Hall.

Tut was waiting for us. He was sitting on his throne and wearing both his pharaoh hat and his fake beard. His face was stony; I couldn't read whether he was happy or angry from his expression.

Wow, I thought. *Whatever he wants, it must be serious if he's dressed up in his king clothes.* Grant had already told me Tut had won the battle, but maybe he was angry because I'd made him go back to camp instead of staying to fight.

Aye was there, too, but his thoughts were easy to read. He hated Grant and me. His eyes shot daggers at us as we walked past him toward the throne. I wondered if it was because I'd taken Tut away from the battle or because I'd saved Tut's life.

"Aston and Grant, you have proven your worth in battle. Against my foes, you have remained true to Egypt, and your blood has been shed to keep her safe. We are grateful for your friendship," Tut said, speaking very formally. It was one of the few times I could remember that he called me by my full name and not the nickname he'd given me, although I truthfully didn't miss being called "Ass."

"We're glad you won, Tut," Grant said.

I nodded. "Yeah, and we're happy you're okay."

"The gods smiled upon us, my friends. Many were not so favored. May Osiris find their hearts worthy of Paradise," Tut said. I could see the sadness in his eyes as he thought about his men who'd died in the battle. "But today is for rejoicing. To celebrate, I have ordered a feast prepared. All the dignitaries in Memphis will be in attendance. It is in your honor, my friends. Go now, and prepare yourselves. I will see you again at the celebration."

We were dismissed. Grant and I exchanged looks as we walked back the way we'd come. A feast? We didn't want to party... we wanted to go home. Somehow, someway, we needed to quit fooling around and get our hands on that amulet today.

The feast was held in the Great Hall. Cushions had been laid over the tile floors, two long lines of them stretching from the double golden doors at the rear of the room all the way up to Tut's throne.

People arrived in a steady stream. Some men wore the usual kilts; some wore shirts as well, or robes over long skirts. Women wore dresses dyed in bright colors.

Everyone wore jewelry—golden necklaces set with green, blue, and red stones, armbands, hair combs, and earrings.

Tut sat on a pile of cushions in front of his throne at the head of the makeshift table. He smiled as a servant escorted us to him. "Welcome, my friends!" he said. He raised his hand and silence instantly descended in the room. "Greet Aston and Grant, friends and heroes of Egypt!"

The crowd cheered, and Grant and I waved as we sat down, one on either side of Tut. I sort of felt like a rock star—the people kept staring at us, and whispering back and forth between themselves. It made me a little uncomfortable as I wondered what they were saying about us.

Tut introduced us to a few people. The only name I recognized was General Horemheb, who had led Tut's troops into battle two days before. He nodded when we were introduced, but his eyes were hard. I realized *he* didn't like us much, either.

A thought hit me then. Had I been wrong about Aye all along? Was it General Horemheb who'd killed Tut? He was a powerful general with the strength of Tut's army behind him. I supposed it would be possible for him to take the throne if Tut was gone.

Maybe it was Aye and Horemheb both, I thought. Maybe they're in it together.

And maybe it was neither of them. The people at the feast were the elite of Egyptian society. Anyone in the room might be wealthy enough or powerful enough to take the throne.

Had we saved Tut from death during the battle only for him to be murdered later? I didn't know the answer. I only hoped we'd planted enough doubt in his mind that he'd be careful and not trust anybody blindly.

Tut was recounting my daring rescue of him during the battle, although I noticed he put a different spin on it. In his version, I merely aided him in destroying the gang of Hittites who were attacking him. According to Tut, he'd been having no real trouble holding his own against them. I supposed he couldn't admit needing help. It wouldn't be good for his god-on-earth image. I also noticed he didn't mention me driving him away from the battle.

I smirked and tried to hide it. To listen to Tut, you'd think he was there until the bitter end.

"My friends, Egypt owes you her gratitude. Name your reward, and I will see it done," Tut said to us.

Grant and I gaped at one another. Reward? Anything? We both knew immediately what we wanted to ask him for... the amulet!

But would he give us his good luck charm? He'd had it since he was an infant, he'd told us.

Well, I thought, there was nothing to be lost by trying. We had to get it somehow, and being given it as a reward was better than stealing it.

"Um, actually, Tut, we sort of like your amulet," I said, pointing to it.

Tut's eyebrows shot up. "My amulet?"

"Yes," Grant chimed in. "We would like to be able to show our president how the great pharaoh of Egypt protects himself from evil."

Good one, Grant, I thought, shooting him a quick smile.

Tut nodded, as if what Grant had said was very wise. "Your presi... presi... king does not wear an amulet?"

We shook our heads. "No, but I think he'd be very

impressed by yours."

Tut ran his fingers over the golden amulet that hung around his neck, tracing the Eye of Ra at its center. "I have worn this since I was a small boy," he said. "It has protected me all of my life." Then he lifted it over his head, and held it up so that everyone could see it. "But today I bestow it upon Grant and Ass in honor of our great friendship." He slipped the amulet over my head.

It was solid gold and felt heavy against my chest. I didn't take the time to admire it, though. Instead, I reached across the table and grabbed Grant's hand, afraid the amulet would take me forward in time without him if we weren't touching.

It didn't.

In fact, it didn't do *anything*.

Had something gone wrong with Merlin's spell? Were Grant and I stuck in ancient Egypt forever?

Chapter Twenty One

Panic soured my stomach and clawed at my nerves. Why were we still in Egypt? We'd done what Merlin had told us to do—we'd gotten the amulet. Why wasn't his spell jerking us forward in time?

I could see Grant was thinking the same thing from the puzzled, scared look on his face. Had Merlin lied to us? Was this his revenge for causing the fire that destroyed his office and all his treasures?

No! No, I would not live out the rest of my days in ancient Egypt. I wanted to go home, even if "home" was the Stanton School for Boys. I wanted to sleep in my own bed. I wanted running water and porcelain toilets. I wanted potato chips and burgers. I wanted a freaking Coke.

"Is something wrong?" Tut asked, arching an eyebrow at me. I realized I was still holding Grant's hand across the table, and was practically hyperventilating. I dropped his hand and jumped to my feet. The room spun; I was still dizzy from the loss of blood. I know that my expression must've been terrified, judging from the concerned look on Tut's face. "What is it, Ass? Are you ill?"

"I... I... yes. Yeah, I'm sick. I need to go lie down. Grant? Come with me, okay?" I mumbled. Fear whipped my thoughts into a tornado, crashing around inside my skull until I was sure it would explode.

"Sure, sure," Grant said. He didn't look any better than I felt. "I feel a little nauseous myself."

:"Go, of course. Seek your rest. Shall I send my physician to you?" Tut asked.

"No, that's okay. We'll be fine," I said as we stood up. "We just..." I couldn't think to finish my sentence. A single question kept rolling through my head, obliterating every other rational thought I might've had. *Why were we still in ancient Egypt?*

"He just needs to rest," Grant finished for me. He jerked his head toward the door, and I followed him out of the Great Hall. Once we were safely in the hallway and away from listening ears, I pulled him to a stop.

"What went wrong? Why are we still here?" I could hear the panic in my voice, making it rise in pitch until it squeaked.

"I don't know!" Grant said. He looked around, but we were alone. "Merlin must've screwed up! What if we're stuck here forever?"

Oh, God... no! I couldn't even *think* about staying here forever! I opened my mouth to say as much, when suddenly the hallway tilted sharply.

My first thought was "Earthquake!" I grabbed for Grant and started to run, thinking only to get out of the palace before it came crashing down on our heads.

Then I felt a familiar tug at my gut, and a sense of seasickness that made my stomach do flip flops. Hot wind buffeted my face, and I glanced at Grant, excitement rising as I realized he was becoming transparent. I knew what was happening, and it curved my lips into a wide grin. Merlin's spell! We were going home!

I was so relieved and happy that I grabbed Grant's

face, even though I could practically see through it, and pulled him to me, kissing him hard. He kissed me back, and I forgot the queasiness in my stomach and the way the hallway was spinning.

Chapter Twenty Two

When I woke up, the only thing I was kissing was the floor of Merlin's classroom.

My head hurt, my stomach still felt sick, but I didn't care. We were home! I pushed up off the floor and sat, immediately looking for Grant.

He was lying next to me, curled on his side. I reached over and gently shook his shoulder. "Wake up, Sleeping Beauty. We're home!"

Grant blinked awake, and I could tell by the slowly widening grin on his face as he realized we were back in our time that he was as happy as I was. I glanced at the big, round clock on the wall above the classroom door, and then at the calendar pinned to the pegboard next to the door. The date was the same as it had been before we'd been thrown back into the past. Holy cow... we'd been in ancient Egypt for days, but only fifteen minutes had passed here!

"Eh-hem."

I looked up as Merlin cleared his throat. He was perched with one hip on the edge of his desk. His smile was smug, and I was suddenly furious with him.

"You!" I snarled. "Do you have any idea what you put us through? We had to go to war, and I got shot by an arrow!" I raised my arm to show him, but to my surprise, both the bandage and the wounds it covered were gone. My skin was smooth and unmarked. There wasn't even a trace of a scar! "What? How?"

Merlin snorted. "The 'what' and 'how' are mine to know and not to share," he said. "And now, I believe you have something that belongs to me." He held out a gnarled, age-spotted hand toward me.

Of course! I'd nearly forgotten about the amulet that hung around my neck. I took it off and handed it to him, although what I really wanted to do was stuff it down his throat until he choked on it.

Merlin smiled as he examined the amulet. He slipped it into a pocket in his jacket, patting it with his hand. "Well done, my boys. Well done."

"Why didn't the amulet take us right back here when we got it?" Grant asked as he sat up next to me. "We thought something went wrong and we'd be stuck back there forever!"

Merlin barked a short, gruff laugh. "Don't be foolish, boy. I *never* make mistakes. It couldn't bring you back here until you were alone. Did you want archeologists to find hieroglyphics depicting you two disappearing in front of witnesses?"

Oh. We hadn't thought of that. It made sense, though. Neither of us wanted to ask how Merlin knew we were at a feast when we received the amulet from Tut. He wouldn't tell us anyway. "Yeah, well, you could've warned us," I grumbled. A thought occurred to me, the one worry that I'd obsessed over ever since meeting Tut. "What about Tut? What happened to him? Was he murdered?" I held my breath, waiting for Merlin's answer.

"No, he was not murdered," Merlin said.

"We did it, then! We saved his life! How old was he

when he died? Did he have children?"

A sad look crept into Merlin's eyes and he held up his hand, cutting off my happy shout. "Didn't I warn you that you can't change the past? That Fate will find a way to achieve her own ends despite your interference? Tut died at the age of nineteen from an infection that set in when he broke his leg. Some think he broke it in battle, others think he was injured during a hunting accident. He left no heirs, and his Grand Vizier took the throne as pharaoh soon after Tut's death."

Anger roiled in my gut. "So it was all for nothing? Aye got his way in the end anyway?"

"No, *Fate* got her way," Merlin corrected. He sighed deeply. "Think of it this way... the past is like a wide, still pond. Throw in even the tiniest pebble, and the ripples it will create will change the face of the water. No one knows how far-reaching those waves might be. Perhaps, had you saved Tut and he lived to a ripe old age, *you* would not have been born." He paused, and then gave us a rare smile. "You did well. You accomplished what you set out to do and returned the amulet to me."

I nodded, but I still felt badly for Tut. In the short time we'd been in Egypt, I'd grown fond of him. We were friends, and even though I knew when I left that I'd never see him again, I felt bad that his life had been cut so short.

Merlin's eyes glittered with sympathy, something I didn't he was capable of feeling until then. "I know it is difficult, but then, I never said it would be easy."

"Gee, thanks. That helps a heap," I said sarcastically.

Merlin cocked one bushy brow. "Mind your tongue or you may find it missing," he snapped.

Now, *that* was more like the Merlin I remembered.

I wasn't done asking questions, though, threat to my

tongue or not. "What about Nefertiti? She went missing while we were there. Did Tut ever find her?"

"She is still somewhat of a mystery. Her tomb was found with her body in it, but it is unknown when she died. Perhaps she did return to the palace after you left, perhaps not. There are some things we may never know," Merlin said. "All we know is that the pharaoh, be it Tutankhamen or Aye, had her mummified and buried as a queen of Egypt."

I opened my mouth to tell Merlin exactly what I thought of his answer, but Grant cut me off.

"Are we done now, Mr. Ambrosius?" Grant asked, shooting me a glare that told me to leave Merlin alone before he zapped us into a pool of quicksand somewhere, or to the top of Mt. Everest without so much as a blanket between us.

"*Done?* Why, my boys, you've only just begun," Merlin answered with a laugh. He went to the shelves built into the classroom wall and pulled out another book. He placed it on his desk and pushed it toward Grant and me. "Attend to the rest of your classes this afternoon, eat dinner, do your homework, and sleep well, because tomorrow is Saturday and I have a full day planned for you two."

I glanced at the title of the book, *Gladiator: We Who Are about to Die Salute You,* and felt my heart speed up. I opened my mouth to protest, but Grant grabbed my elbow and pulled me away. "See you tomorrow, Mr. Ambrosius," he said, forcing me out of the classroom and into the hallway.

The classroom door slowly swung closed behind us all by itself.

"Did you see the title...?" I asked him.

"Yeah, I saw."

"Is he crazy? He can't send us *there*!"

"Oh, I think he can. Can, and *will*," Grant replied.

With another backward glance at the closed door to Ambrosius' history room, I nodded resignedly and followed Grant down the hallway toward our next class, Physics.

I could swear I heard Merlin's laughter following us all the way there.

Repeating History: The Eye of Ra